The Operator

by

Nicholas Orr

The Operator

by

Nicholas Orr
Copyright 2018
All Rights Reserved

Generally speaking, the Way of the warrior is resolute acceptance of death.

Study strategy over the years and achieve the spirit of the warrior. Today is victory over yourself of yesterday; tomorrow is your victory over lesser men.

- Miyamoto Musashi,
military philosopher and the greatest swordsman in the history of Japan

ONE

The black lab at his feet walked in a circle three times and laid down. *How tired would a dog have to be for them to skip the walking in circles routine?* Thomas Thrasher wondered to himself. Sarge was Tommy's five-year-old black lab and companion for as many years. Originally, Thrasher had named the pup "Sergeant Sizemore" after one of his Infantry School mentors. That name, of course, was quickly shortened to Sarge for convenience sake.

Sarge had the telltale Labrador "blockhead", large paws for swimming and was pure black, so much so that he was practically invisible at night. Of his character traits, Sarge was a mouth-breather, no surprise there, snored to beat the band, and on the frequent occasion he produced audible flatulence which never ceased to surprise him.

Thomas Thrasher had grown up in a household that always had at least one family dog present. Periodically, against their better judgement, Tommy's parents had allowed a second or third dog to live with them. That situation was most often the result of pleading and pestering from Tommy's younger brother and sister.

As Sarge settled in for a mid-afternoon nap at his master's feet, Thomas Thrasher toasted the tip of a Fuente "Hemingway" cigar and then slowly puffed to bring the stick to life. As a companion to the cigar, a dark Italian roast cup of coffee steamed close by. The Macbook in his lap showed the slight ash traces of a hundred cigars before. Dog and master were lounging on the wooden deck off of the back of the house. Though he loved premium cigars, Tommy never smoked them indoors, with the exception of the attached garage. Besides, the late September weather was near perfect, 70 degrees or so, and little to no wind.

This afternoon's mission was simply to sort through the emails that Thomas had not gotten to yet and answer those that merited a response. Even though he received email notifications on his iPhone, Thrasher found it much simpler to type responses with a real keyboard. The vast majority of inbound electronic correspondence was business related, few friends or acquaintances took the time to craft an email anymore, deferring instead to a text message or some form of chat. For that reason, he was surprised to see *Tommy I need help* in the title bar of one message.

His spam/junk mail filter did a very good job of blocking the phishing, trolling, and "slut-spam", as Tommy called it, out of his inbox, so he thought it might be a legitimate message. The address from the "Tommy I need help" email was unfamiliar but Thrasher figured as long as he didn't open any attachments he'd be safe from "cyber-herpes", his term for spyware, malware, viruses, etc.

Thrasher clicked open the email and realized immediately that it was a legitimate correspondence written by a real person; no hyperlinks embedded in the text, no banners or other pictures to click on, just a short message.

Tommy,

I know it's been a long time and I know we didn't part on the best of terms, but I don't know who else to turn to. I'm scared and I think I might be in danger. I know emails aren't really secure and I'm afraid to say too much here.

Can we talk face to face? My mobile is 702 -555-1779

Beth

Thrasher took a long pull on the Hemingway and blew the fragrant smoke toward the sky. Beth, or Elizabeth Alexander, had broken his heart. The thought that he had once been so young and so smitten with a girl made him laugh out loud. The sound of his laughter caused Sarge to stir from his nap, but only for a moment.

The way he viewed it, Beth was a part of a different life, a life before the Marine Corps, before he had seen combat, before he had visited so much of the world, both beautiful and ugly. That love-struck, heart-broken version of Tommy Thrasher did not even seem like the same person he was today.

It had been eight, no nine years, since Tommy had seen Beth in person. During the long quiet hours that always accompanied his overseas deployments, his thoughts would drift back to the old Tommy, the young naive one who thought he was going to marry Beth. Their time together had been like a wild roller coaster ride.

The passion of youth had taken ahold of them both. They made love with the ferocious energy that young people have. Tommy and Beth were each the most serious relationship that the other one had ever had. However, people change when they stop being teenagers and enter their twenties, they want different things and many thoughts and ideas that were once critically important become trivial.

The honest answer that Tommy had settled on years earlier was that they both grew together and then apart. The damning fact was that she realized it long before he did, or at least before he was ready to admit it to himself. When Beth ended their time together it was a hard gut punch to Thrasher. The ache of that gut punch lasted until he arrived at Parris Island, South Carolina for Marine Corps Basic Training. Becoming a United States Marine was all that Recruit Thrasher could or would allow himself to focus on from that point forward.

The Global War on Terror had been underway in earnest for two years and Tommy had no illusions that his decision to enlist in the Marine Corps as an Infantryman would lead to anything but combat overseas. *Hell*, he thought, *boot camp seems like another lifetime ago.*

Taking a sip of the coffee that was beginning to cool, the seasoned Marine forced himself back to the present. What the hell was this cryptic letter from Beth all about? If she was really in danger, why not just call the police? If it was a real emergency, there was 9-1-1. Who or what had frightened her to the point where she feared that her emails would be compromised? And, after all these years, of all the people that Elizabeth Alexander had to know, why reach out to him? Thrasher grabbed a pen and copied the mobile number in the little notebook he kept closeby. Under the number he scratched out one word; *Kitten.* Then he deleted the email and powered down the Macbook.

If you know the enemy and know yourself you need not fear the results of a hundred battles.

Sun Tzu

TWO

Tommy woke to Sarge's wet nose poking him in the face. "You are worse than rooster." Thrasher said to the Lab who began pacing back and forth at the side of the bed. "Alright, alright, I'm coming."

Thrasher rarely set an alarm clock when he was at home. Sarge would sense the sunrise and pester his master until he was up and ready for their morning walk. Even though he did have a fenced in backyard, Tommy was in the habit of taking Sarge for a morning walk and then again most evenings. He did not mind so much. The morning walks helped to get the blood flowing at the start of the day. Also, walking the dog seemed like a simple and civilized thing to do. Having spent so much of his time either on military bases or deployed to the field, Thrasher appreciated the simple pleasure of taking a dog for a walk.

The next part of their routine was breakfast. By the time they had returned home the coffee maker had finished brewing. Tommy would prepare his breakfast while Sarge sat and watched him intently. The Black Lab knew from experience that something good was coming. Thrasher was a bachelor, so most mornings it was just the two of them for breakfast. The Marine would put one or two extra eggs in the pan for Sarge. If he was in a rush, Tommy would just crack a raw egg into the

Lab's food bowl, but there was plenty of time for a cooked meal this morning.

As he consumed his breakfast and coffee, Thrasher checked his email inbox with his iPhone. No new messages from the address that Beth had used were present. There were a couple emails that he would need to respond to, but nothing that required his immediate attention. Next he looked at the weather app and then the news. Tommy looked at the overseas news with a different perspective than the average American. Trouble in a foreign country often led to protection detail assignments and open contracts that needed people with his skill set to fill.

The day's schedule was open. There were no appointments or commitments that required his attention. Tommy had some chores to do around the house and then he would head to the gym.

Thrasher hated running. When he played high school football he had run innumerable laps around the practice field in the heat of summer. Marines run and they run a lot. Thrasher had run in the sweltering southern heat of South Carolina on Parris Island and North Carolina at Camp Lejeune. He ran in the high Mojave Desert country of 29 Palms. He had run overseas in the jungle heat of Okinawa, on the deck of the flat top troop transport ships, in the arid heat of the Arabian desert. Though it was a stretch, Tommy used to joke that he had run enough during his time in the Corps to navigate the globe.

Now that no one was forcing him to run, Tommy ran only on a treadmill in the gym when he felt the need. That is not to say that he ignored his physical fitness. While working on contract for an "Other Government Agency", OGA, Thrasher was introduced by a teammate to serious barbell training and he enjoyed that far more than endless push ups, pull ups, and sit ups.

It was tough to find a functional barbell gym overseas, but one of the perks of working for OGA was that they were able to find and acquire things that a standard grunt could not. Now that he was back in CONUS (Continental United States), Thrasher took advantage of modern strength and fitness centers with shiny barbells, rubber padded Olympic weight plates and blessed air conditioning.

As he chalked up his hands in preparation for the deadlift portion of his training routine, Tommy caught glimpse of someone that sent a rush of blood from his large muscle groups to a more sensitive region. Connie Stanley, the former Mrs. Kurt Stanley, was lingering over by the padded mat, workout area where the personal trainers held their classes.

Connie, had been divorced from Mr. Stanley for not quite two years and part of her plan for independence included getting back in shape. That she had done, and quite well. Her black yoga pants appeared to be painted onto her fit and toned legs and firm well rounded bottom. She wore a peach colored tank top that allowed her beige sports bra to peek out in certain places. The sports bra fought to restrain her ample bosom and keep "the twins" in place during her workouts.

Thrasher turned his attention away from Connie instinctively knowing that if he gazed too long it would have a negative impact on his concentration for the deadlift. There was 405 pounds on the deadlift bar and that steel would not be satisfied until Tommy has lifted it five times in succession. If he lost focus, he could fail in his attempt or strain one or more muscles. The discipline of years of hard training took over and he set himself over the bar.

As he reached full extension on pull number five, Thrasher let out an audible grunt, relaxed and allowed the weight to descend in a controlled crash down onto the rubber padded lifting platform. His chest heaved and he sucked in oxygen to bring his heartbeat back to normal. Looking over toward the deadlift jack, he needed to remove the plates and put the bar away, Tommy saw Connie sitting on a bench watching him.

"Hey stranger" she called. "Need a hand putting those away." Satisfied that he had completed the training session, deadlifting was always the last exercise, Thrasher allowed a smile and relaxed as the blood moved back down there. "If you think you can handle it." he joked.

"Don't you worry tough guy, this girl can handle it." Connie was smiling a playful grin as she walked up to the platform. Her blond hair glistened from the perspiration she had worked up during her workout. Thrasher took in the whole picture and thought, not for the first time, what a fool Kurt Stanley was for letting her get away.

Connie's apartment was walking distance from the gym so Tommy left his Dodge Ram 2500 in the lot. As she closed the apartment door behind her, Connie asked, "Together or separately?" "Oh, definitely together." Tommy responded. He had already dropped his gym bag containing his street clothes, flat-soled squat shoes, weight lifting belt, and a Glock 19 onto the floor. Before exiting the fitness center he had slipped on his tennis shoes. He always deadlifted in socks only.

Connie disrobed first. With adept skill she slipped off her crossfit shoes, peeled off the yoga pants revealing a tantalizing black thong, and removed the tank top and sports bra in one motion.

By the time Tommy entered the bathroom she had already started the shower and was warming the water. There was no tub, but a large, clear glass shower stall. From experience, Thrasher knew there was plenty of room for two in the stall. As the glass walls began to steam, he joined Connie under the warm waterfall.

Grabbing a bar of her lavender scented soap, Thrasher took over. Connie stood motionless with her back to him as he lathered the soap in his hands and went to work. Tommy started on her back and shoulders, soaping up her soft skin with his firm, strong hands. She let out a deep sigh and braced herself against the shower wall when his hands reach her bottom, a bottom she was proud to have worked on so diligently.

Reaching around, Thrasher took each breast in his hands lathering them top to bottom taking special care to tease her now fully erect nipples. "Mmm, I have missed you." she managed to say between deep breathes. Wordlessly, he moved his right hand down to her belly, rubbing it gently and pausing. "Don't tease." she said, barely loud enough for him to hear over the running water. With a bit of lather remaining on his palm, Thrasher eased his hand down between her legs and felt the soft golden blond hair that she took care to keep trimmed. Her breathing grew deeper and the sighs more desperate as he soaped and lathered between her gloriously soft thighs.

Spinning around, she wrapped him with both arms, pressed her wet body against him and coiled one leg around both of his like a constrictor. "I think I'm clean enough now, said said "and besides, it looks like he is ready."

Lying atop the sheets in Connie's queen-sized bed, Tommy gazed at the slowly spinning ceiling fan. Her head was resting on his chest covered with thick brown hair and he could sense her breathing long and deep. She had dozed off and he allowed himself to smile and enjoy moment.

Thomas Thrasher had met Connie Stanley, she didn't see a point changing her last name after the split, six months earlier at the gym. She was five years his senior, but that mattered not at all to him. From the beginning, they had mutually agreed to "keep things simple". Her marriage had lasted seven years and she was still leary of a committed relationship. Thrasher traveled a good bit due to his work and was perfectly willing to take what she was willing to give.

Both had also agreed, while sharing a bottle of wine, that the term "fuck buddy" was childish and something that millennials said, so they would not use it. But, they were indeed friends with serious benefits. She didn't text him incessantly or try to keep tabs on him which would have been the dealbreaker he never had to address. Connie had never even been to his home which was a bit of a shame, Sarge would probably love her.

She also didn't mind that he was hairy, a product of his Scottish ancestry. Modern millennial girls were too obsessed with having their men shave or "manscape", a term that made Tommy want to puke. He was a man, a real man and he wanted a woman who desired and appreciated that.

Thrasher viewed the post-workout romps in Connie's apartment as a bit of payback that the universe had gifted to him for all of the long deployments where he had gone without the comfort of a woman. While so many of his high school classmates were getting drunk and screwing like rabbits in college, Tommy had been overseas fighting the forces of Islamic fundamentalism so that they could keep on living oblivious to the dangers of the real world.

When he occasionally communicated with those old classmates, none could really understand what he had been through or what he had done. Tommy was an oddity to them, a strange animal that they saw but could not really comprehend. Having been in combat and lost several friends to war, Thrasher would say that trying to explain real combat to someone who had never experienced it was akin to explaining sex to a virgin. You could talk all you wanted, but unless you had actually experienced it, you could not truly understand what it was like.

He sensed that Connie had woken from her post-coital slumber. She lifted her head and looked into his blue eyes. "I don't know about you, but I am starving." she said. "I could eat, he responded, "and I think we both need the protein."

THREE

It had been twenty-four hours since the email from Beth Alexander. Wary of making a decision based upon emotion, Tommy had deliberately given himself time to consider the situation. He had engaged in a strenuous workout at the gym, as well as a fortuitous session at Connie's apartment. Certainly he had time to consider the message with a clear head, Thrasher convinced himself.

Life experience had taught Tommy that emotional decisions were dangerous ones. He was also cautious about buying into other people's problems. Hard lessons had shown him that life will offer enough challenges and risks without you having to buy into the problems of others.

He was sitting at his dark stained, hardwood desk and he pulled open the deep drawer on the right hand side. The draw had originally been designed with a rack to hold a series of hanging cardboard folders, but no one used paper files and file folders anymore. From the deep drawer he removed a gray steel lockbox. After he had keyed the lock, Tommy removed a generic looking, black mobile phone, the kind that you can pay cash for at the local discount store and put "minutes" on with a prepaid phone card, also secured with cash.

It took a few moments for the phone to power up completely. When the signal showed full strength,

Thrasher typed in the number he had saved in the notebook and completed a simple text;

Kitten, When and Where? Tiger

He pushed the green send button and waited. If someone was indeed monitoring her phone they might read the message but they would have no way to link it back to him directly. The last thing he wanted was an angry, estranged husband looking to put him in his place.

While awaiting an answer, he had no idea how long it would take, Thrasher opened his laptop computer and reviewed a couple of open contracts and potential assignments in his email box. Tommy had transitioned directly from active duty Marine Corps to Military Contractor where he had proven himself as a valuable asset to various OGA contract officers.

His contracts and assignments now were sporadic, some were short term a week or two, and other lasted for months. Unlike many of the contractors he had worked with, who blew through their big money like it was their last week on earth, Tommy had put away a good deal and even invested some of it. He was a silent partner in one business with his friend, Matty, a bass player and songwriter for a successful rock band. Working with Matty, Thrasher had become a partner/investor in a high end tattoo emporium that also displayed and sold some pretty wild original paintings.

The tattoo/art studio didn't bring in Rockefeller money, but it was a "diversified revenue stream". Tommy had learned about the idea of diversified revenue from an older and wiser former Special Forces Team Sergeant. The old 18Z (pronounced Eighteen Zulu, the US Army designation for SF Team Sergeant) was near the end of his operating career had strongly advising the younger Thrasher to invest the money he was making in things other than guns and ammo, or "coke and hookers" as most of them joked.

None of the "Clearance Jobs" that Tommy reviewed looking enticing enough for him to go through the pain in the ass of overseas travel again. Clearance Jobs were those available only to personnel who had already received and maintained an United States Department of Defense "Security Clearance" such as "Secret" or "Top Secret". The "Confidential" clearance was the lowest level and from Thrasher's perspective was given out like candy. Tommy had originally gained a "Secret" clearance in the Corps and then he was able to elevate that to "Top Secret" when he went to work as a contractor.

A Top Secret or TS in the military contracting world was the golden ticket for high paying assignments and Thrasher was extremely careful to maintain it. A DUI, or even a misdemeanor charge for fighting in public could tank his TS clearance. Therefore he acquitted himself accordingly and was a well-behaved barbarian while CONUS.

Sarge had begun to pace around the office and make needy growling sounds. Looking at his watch, Tommy realized it has already late afternoon, the black lab's belly was growling. "Okay buddy, let's get you some chow." he said and Sarge happily followed him into the kitchen.

After dinner, Tommy and Sarge retired to the back porch. Thrasher torched a hand-rolled Dominican cigar and tossed a tennis ball for the lab. After retrieving it only twice, Sarge decided that he had enough and laid down. "You lazy, old bastard." Tommy mockingly scolded. Sergeant Sizemore paid no attention and commenced licking himself.

After returning home from one of his first Contract Deployments, Thrasher has accepted an invitation from a teammate and fellow contractor, Josh Kimball, to visit him in Salt Lake City, Utah. Thrasher, having been born in Michigan had never been out west until he trained at 29 Palms Marine Corps base in the Mojave Desert. He did not really like the desert but he did love the American west, especially the mountains. He fell in love with the SLC area and had decided to relocate there a few years prior. His house was in the adjoining city of West Valley.

Thrasher examined the cigar as light gray smoke drifted from the tip. He had a few true cigar buddies, men who genuinely appreciated a premium cigar. Most of his old buddies and friends referred to the machine-made garbage that they sold at the gas station as "cigars". They did not understand the difference nor appreciate it. Matty was one of the few who genuinely appreciated the finer points of the enjoyment hand-rolled cigars.

Tommy picked up his phone and sent a text;

What's up rock star?

The response was a mobile phone picture of Matty, smiling with a cigar in his teeth. Then the words;

Relaxing, Go on stage in an hour.

Thrasher texted back;

Kick some ass, talk next week?

Roger that.

Tommy had what he considered a handful of true, genuine friends. Regardless of how long it had been since they saw each other, they could pick up right where they left off. None of them got weird or butt-hurt if the other did not call or text frequently. Often Tommy would send one sentence or even a one word text out of the blue. *I like cheese,* was one of my many go to one-liners. The response would be *Ha!* or the "thumbs up" symbol.

He did indeed want to talk with Matty during the next week. As a silent partner in the Tattoo/Art studio, Thrasher would talk with Matty about once every four to six weeks. Thrasher was overdue for a face to face visit with Matthew Delvecchio, or "Matty D" as he was know in the Rock and Roll world.

Between Tommy traveling for contracts and Matty's touring schedule with his band, Solid Gold Cadillac or SGC, it was tough to be in the same place at the same time. Thrasher puffed his cigar and made the mental commitment to check the calendar and work out a visit soon.

Whenever Tommy and Matty would get together there would be three primary items on the agenda. First they would knock out the business talk about the studio; profits, losses, new ventures, etc. Then there would be range time. Unlike many of those in the music business, Matty was a serious gun guy and 2nd Amendment supporter. Between the two, Thrasher and Delvecchio would put hundreds rounds down range when they had the chance.

Last on the agenda, but just as important as all the rest, there would be cigar time. Sometimes the business talk would be mixed with cigar time, but it was just as important to the two friends to share some quality bonding time over a couple of premium hand-rolled cigars, a dark roast coffee or perhaps an adult beverage or two.

Occasionally, Thrasher would get together with Matty when SGC was on the road touring. If the show was within driving distance, Tommy would meet the tour bus at the venue. After sound check was complete, they would duck out to a local cigar bar, if one was convenient. Tommy laughed aloud thinking of the strange looks they would get. The two of them were certainly an odd pair. Thrasher was clean shaven with a high and tight haircut, Delvecchio looked very much the part of the rockstar; long hair and beard, tattoos and piercings. Despite their outward appearances, they were very much alike where it counted.

FOUR

He woke unusually early. Normally his alarm clock was Sarge sticking his wet nose into Tommy's face so he could go out and relieve himself. Thrasher laid in bed, looking toward the ceiling in a darkened room. The faint sounds of the black lab snoring could be heard from the floor at the foot of the bed.

Rather than attempt to go back to sleep, he decided to get a jump on the day. He slipped quietly out of bed hoping to get the coffee pot started before his furry companion woke for his morning walk. Sneaking past the slumbering K9 like a parent not wanting to wake the baby, Tommy found his way to the kitchen without turning on a light and pushed the start button on the DeLonghi stainless steel combination coffee and espresso maker.

As was his habit, he had set up the coffee maker before bed so it would be ready to go in the morning. Though he rarely used the espresso option, Tommy did enjoy the luxury of being able to offer the occasional guest a fresh espresso if they desired. One of his buddies from the Corp has teased him about spending so much on a coffee maker, "I can get eight coffee makers from PriceMart for what you paid for that."

Long deployments overseas had taught Thrasher the value of good coffee. He had experienced some of the best coffee he had ever tasted while traveling through Europe and soon adopted the mantra that, "Life is too short for bad coffee". Tommy had learned that the reason discount store coffee makers produced such average, bland coffee was because they never got the water hot enough. When it came time to purchase his own appliance for the house, he opted for quality over price.

As the last bit of coffee dripped into the pot, the machine gave off the familiar gurgling sound and that was all Sarge needed to hear. The lab trotted into the kitchen eager for his morning walk and an opportunity to drain his bladder.

Most mornings during their a.m. exercise, Sarge and Tommy would encounter some of the local citizens out for their morning dog-walking ritual. Mrs. Jones, at least he thought it was Jones, a fifty something woman, would be out with her French bulldog, Gigi. Gigi barked at Sarge attempting to establish dominance but the Black Lab paid her little mind. Another neighbor, man likely in his mid-forties, who Tommy knew only as "glasses and receding hairline" often walked a friendly Chocolate Lab named that he called "Buddy". Buddy was always happy to greet Tommy and Sarge.

It struck Tommy how the small dogs were always the *yappiest* and most annoying, while the larger dogs were most playful and friendly. He guessed that in the animal kingdom, like the human world, the small ones were always trying to compensate by being noisy and overly aggressive.

On their return lap, Sarge alerted to a dog/owner combination headed their direction. Tommy instinctively took a firm hold on the Black Lab's leash not knowing what to expect from the new animal. Holding the lead on a golden brown and white Corgi was a young lady in running shorts, a pink t-shirt and cushioned athletic shoes. Thrasher couldn't imagine that the stubby legs of the Corgi would do very much running. "Good morning" he greeted the two as they approached.

Tommy stopped walking and held Sarge's leash so they could make the approach. The Corgi seemed friendly enough and didn't bark. "Her name is Lady." the woman offered "She's okay with other dogs." Lady and Sarge engaged in the sniffing each other out routine.

"He is Sarge and I'm Tommy." Thrasher offered his right hand as he controlled the excited lab with his left. "I'm Lynne" she said pausing a bit awkwardly as her right hand held Lady's leash. Lynne reached over with her left hand for a quick handshake. "We're here staying with my mom, just down the street." she related. "It's nice to meet you." "Nice to meet you too, the Marine/Contractor said. "Sarge and I get our exercise most mornings, maybe we'll see you again." "That would be nice." Lynne smiled and coaxed Lady away from the sniffing ritual and headed away.

Thrasher snuck a quick glance over his shoulder as the departed. Lynne had shoulder length auburn hair that waved in the slight morning breeze. The rear view was just as good as the front view he thought, then turned his attention to getting back home.

Sarge had eaten his breakfast, taken his morning walk, and now it was time to retire to his favorite spot on the rug for morning nap. It was still relatively early so Thrasher decided to hit the outdoor shooting range. The retired guys who spent more time talking than shooting normally arrived after 9am and the younger guys with day jobs would show up in the afternoon. Thrasher liked to get in his training session when no one else was around. Many times Tommy would deliberately train in the rain, knowing that 99.9 percent of shooters would never stand in the rain to engage in a hobby.

His range bag with loaded magazines was always ready to go so it took little time to prep the silver Dodge Ram. Within twenty minutes Tommy punched in the four digit code into the range's keypad. The electronic gate whined as it slid open via a large chain mechanism. His bet had been right. As he made his way down to the "U" shaped berm of the 50 yard pistol range, not another vehicle was in sight.

Dropping the tailgate on the 2500 pickup truck, Tommy drew his Glock 19 pistol from the concealed carry holster. He swapped out the expanding hollow-point ammunition for a magazine filled with less expensive full-metal jacket ammo and returned the black semi-automatic pistol to the hybrid Kydex and Leather gun sheath.

From a soft-sided black nylon case, Thrasher withdrew his AR-15 rifle. It was essentially the same as the M4 he carried overseas, minus the "fun switch" that would allow fully automatic fire. Raising the gun to his shoulder he looked through the Aimpoint Micro T1 optic. The red aiming dot was glowing just like it should be. The T1 Micro had a battery life of 50,000 hours so Tommy never bothered to turn it off, he just kept it set on the middle brightness setting.

Thirty minutes later, the range was littered with approximately 100 pieces of empty 5.56mm brass and nearly 50 pieces of 9mm brass. Thrasher ran through a series of shooting exercises to keep his skills sharp, first engaging with the rifle and then transitioning immediately to the pistol whenever the 30 round magazines of the rifle went dry.

He was picking up the brass when he spotted a white pickup truck followed by a dark blue sedan coming down the range drive. *Perfect timing,* he thought.

On the trip home Tommy decided to stop at "The Armory", an indoor gun range and full service gun shop. Only on rare occasion did Tommy use the indoor range. Thanks to the behavior of "amatuer fucktards" there were so many Range Rules that Thrasher could not practice ninety percent of what he needed to in order to keep his skills sharp.

Charlie was at the counter. Thrasher liked Charlie. Unlike most gun store clerks, Charlie actually knew what he hell he was talking about and didn't try to bullshit people when they were looking for guns and gear. From Tommy's experience, too many gun store clerks were focused on pushing useless crap on the under-educated gun buyers who came in.

"Hey, Charlie." Thrasher called out as he approached the counter. "How's my favorite shooter?" Charlie responded. "I'm doing better than I deserve. Tommy kidded, "I need to order some more nine and five-five-six." Charlie was only half-teasing when he called Tommy his "favorite shooter". Thrasher was a good customer for a gun shop. He only haggled on occasion, didn't bitch about the cost of quality gear and every month to six weeks he would by at least one case of 9mm and one case of 5.56mm NATO or .223 Remington training ammunition. Cases of ammunition held 1000 rounds each.

"I'm guessing you want the usual order?" Charlie inquired. "Yep." "I'll order it and it will be two or three days. You want to pay now?" Tommy pulled out his wallet and handed Charlie his debit card. He was a very good customer.

Upon returning home, Thrasher went through his ritual of recharging the rifle and pistol magazines. His Glock 19 had been reloaded with the "killer" hollow-point ammo before he stepped off of the range. He showered and shaved. As he wiped the remaining remnants of shaving cream from his face, Thrasher smiled recalling the facial hair changes he'd been through.

As a United States Marine, Tommy had to maintain grooming standards, even in the field. While in the woods, jungle, or desert, Thrasher would use his stainless steel canteen cup as a sink and hold his emergency signal mirror in his left hand and a plastic disposable razor in his right.

Tommy had shaved every single day of his Marine Corps career and had longed for a time that he could relax and grown his hair out. Before he had checked in to his first Military Contractor assignment Tommy was pleased to receive an email that stated "Relaxed Grooming Standards, Stop Shaving, all Team Members will wear beards".

In the Arabic culture, all men wore beards. A man without a beard was viewed as a boy. And so, since they worked with and around the locals, Tommy kept a beard, sometimes trimmed neatly, sometimes wild, the entire time he contracted overseas. Now that he was CONUS, he had decided to go back to being clean-shaven.

With just a towel wrapped around his waist, Thrasher walked into the office and checked the disposable "burner" phone. Before he picked up the phone he could see the tiny amber light blinking on the face, it meant there was a message. One text was available and it read;

Tiger,

Thank you so much for reaching back to me. Can we meet soon? The sooner the better. Please let me know. Text me anytime, day or night.

Kitten

Well, there it was. In the back of his mind Tommy had wondered if Beth would even respond. But, now she had so he was committed. In his previous life, the two had given each other pet names. He had called her his Kitten and she in kind called him her Tiger. He had wondered if she would even remember, after all it had been not quite ten years.

I hate giving advice, because people won't take it.

Jack Nicholson

FIVE

Tommy, despite his best efforts over the years, had not completely flushed Beth Alexander from his mind. Through mutual friends he had made casual inquiries over the years. She had married while he was in the Corps. One late evening, after one too many adult beverages, he was ashamed to admit to himself that he had stalked her on Facebook. She had relocated from Ohio with her husband to the city of Henderson, Nevada, a town just south of Las Vegas, at least according to her Facebook profile. Apparently her husband had a job working for one of the hotel casinos out there.

After the shameful Facebook stalking occurrence, Thrasher told himself he was better than that and did not do it again. That had been over a year ago, but it was a safe bet she still lived out there.

He took a deep breath, picked up the mobile phone and typed,

Still in Henderson?

Then hit, the send button.

Not five minutes went by and phone vibrated and the amber light flashed.

Yes, yes I am. When and where?

Now the die had truly been cast. He couldn't with good conscience ignore the previous email or text. Tommy, like most other contractors flush with overseas cash had been to Las Vegas on more than one occasion. Once, he and several of his old Marine Corps buddies had met up there to trade "no shit, there I was" stories, drink too much and live like kings if only for a short while.

Thrasher knew that Henderson was a six hour drive from SLC down US Interstate 15. He had no intention of flying, too much TSA bullshit and there no way he was traveling unarmed. The only time he deliberately disarmed himself was when he was forced to fly to another country and then he would be armed up as soon as he landed and met up with the contract officer and his team.

Tommy would need to make arrangements for Sarge, which would be relatively easy. Josh babysat Sarge often and the old Lab got along famously with Josh's German Shepherd, Reagan.

First a called was placed to Josh. His friend assured him that Sarge was alway welcome, anytime. Tommy thanked his friend and made arrangements to drop Sarge off after breakfast the next day.

Back to the burner phone.

Tomorrow afternoon

I'll text this when I'm in town and tell you where.
Talk soon

This time the phone buzzed almost immediately.

Thank you. Be safe.

Even if it turned out to be nothing, a marital disagreement or some such thing, there was no way Thrasher was turning around and making a six hour drive right back to SLC. He needed to find overnight lodging. He had no way of knowing how long he'd be in Henderson, he had told Josh that he would be gone for two days, maybe three. Ten minutes later he had a room booked for two nights at the Hilton Garden Inn in Henderson. He didn't need anything fancy, but he also did not want to stay at some discount motel where tweekers were cooking meth in the room next door.

As Tommy dressed himself, he went over a mental checklist of what he needed to do and what he needed to take with him. This was not that difficult of a task as he traveled so often.

Walking over to the safe in his office, he worked the combination and then counted out $1000 in hundreds and twenties. Tommy had no expectation of using that much money for the trip, but he was also seasoned enough not to rely solely on plastic cards or risk running low on cash.

He packed his overnight bag and set out everything he thought he would need, including the burner phone and the crappy generic charger that had come with it. All his preparations were made and all of his gear was ready and it was not even noon yet. Taking a moment to relax it occurred to him just how hungry he was.

Picking up his personal iPhone, Thrasher sent Connie a text,

Lunch or Dinner?

She replied after a couple of minutes.

Too busy for lunch, how about dinner? Usual place at 6?

Tommy took a lot of his meals alone, but he liked to have company whenever he could get it.

Dinner would be great. See you at 6.

To the kitchen he went. For lunch it would be a handmade sandwich with Sarge as his dining companion.

At five minutes to six Tommy pulled into the parking lot of the restaurant that had become their usual place. It was located minutes from Connie's apartment and served breakfast, lunch, and dinner. It also stayed open until 10 p.m. on the weekdays and 11 p.m. weeknights which had come in quite handy.

Entering the restaurant Tommy did a quick glance for Connie. She was not in sight so he asked the hostess for a table for two. It was a weekday evening so the place was not too busy. There was a table with four men in business suits, two man/woman couples in booths and one woman seated alone in a booth. Thrasher had been to the eatery at least ten, perhaps twelve times before. He was familiar with the location of the emergency exits, the kitchen entrance and bathroom location.

As a matter of professional habit, Thrasher inspected every new building he entered for the emergency or alternate exit. In a crisis; fire, robbery, whatever, the majority of people would instinctively default to the way they entered the building. That fact essentially guaranteed a panicked log jam of people at the main entrance during an emergency.

The hostess and the waitstaff all looked familiar and nothing appeared out of the ordinary on this evening. Tommy glanced at his phone for a possible message from Connie, but found none. Seven minutes later she walked through the front door, spotted him and made a straight line for the table. He was out of his seat standing as she arrived

"Sorry, she said, "I had a showing and the traffic turned to shit." She offered her cheek and he dutifully kissed it then pulled out her chair. "No big deal, I only just arrived myself." he assured her. Connie was wearing a soft teal business dress. She was a real estate agent for a local broker and had obviously come straight from work.

She continued, "Today was the second time I showed that house to the same couple. They are dragging their feet for whatever reason. They've looked at every square inch of the property, twice. If they ask for a third showing they can fuck off." Tommy laughed out loud at her blunt profanity. "Really?" he asked with a sarcastic tone. "No, not really. Connie admitted. "My boss would can me for sure if I turned away a potential buyer. But, it felt good saying that outloud." "Consider me your personal confessor my dear, everything you say stays right here."

Connie shook her head as she laughed at him. "Okay, Monsignor, how about we order some food, I'm starving." Tommy waved his hand and the waitress came right over.

After they had finished their food, Thrasher excused himself to the restroom. He paused at the register to pay their check on the way back. When he had entered and saw the woman sitting alone he assumed she was waiting for someone to join her.

No one had and he noticed she was reading a book as she slowly took her meal.

Thrasher instructed the hostess to put the lone woman's meal on his check. She seemed puzzled and said "You're sure." "Yes, quite sure." he assured her. Tommy ate alone often enough. He figured it would be a pleasant surprise and act of kindness would brighten her evening. It certainly wasn't a daily occurrence, but he had anonymously paid for the meal of a lone stranger on several occasions.

Returning to the table with Connie he didn't bother taking his seat. She was finished and sipping her water awaiting his return. "Check's paid. Let's get out of here." he said. That was all the prompting she needed. In the lot she invited him to her apartment for a quick drink. "Just a quick drink. Nothing else?" he teased. "Don't be an ass. Connie scolded with a smile on her face. "I might be tired."

Connie was not a scotch drinker, but she kept a bottle of Glenlivet 15 on hand for Tommy's evening visits. He never drank during the daytime after their workout sessions, but he would take drink in the evening under a more relaxed setting.

The former Mrs. Stanley poured herself a generous glass of Cabernet and handed him a scotch tumbler with the Glenlivet, neat, no ice. Then took a seat next to him on her comfy leather sofa.

"I've been on my feet all day. Would you be a sweetie?" she asked hopefully. "Yes, of course my dear." "Goodie!" she squealed. In a flash she had slipped off her high heeled shoes, shifted on the couch and placed her feet gently in his lap. He dutifully began to rub her tired feet. Connie kept her toes painted and took regular pedicures. Today the toenail polish was a shade of dark red. Thrasher felt the blood moving to his manhood as he rubbed her pretty feet and toes. They were soft and slender and he was not ashamed that the act turned him on.

"Oh, you are an angel." Connie sighed then took a long sip of the wine. "Where were you seven years ago?" "Killing haj." he replied bluntly and immediately regretted it. *Killing haj* was not really something you said to a citizen, particularly a lady. Connie seemed unfazed. "Well, for a killer you sure do give a wonderful foot rub." He took the cue. "Didn't you know, all us barbarians give great foot massages."

"Why should I be surprised? You certainly are a barbarian in there." Connie smiled as she nodded her head toward the bedroom. "I thought you said that you were tired." Tommy feigned surprise. "I said 'I might be tired' not that I was for certain. A lady can change her mind. That is her prerogative."

"Yes, that is true. It is your prerogative. Now I'm going to exercise mine." Thrasher swept her feet from his lap. He stood up from the couch and took the wine glass from her hand placing it carefully on the end table. In one deliberate move he scooped her up off of the couch and held her aloft in his strong arms.

Once in her bedroom clothing was discarded rapidly. She stood facing him, though her head came only to his chest. Official Marine Corps records stated that Thrasher, Thomas, H. stood 73 and ¼ inches. He reached up and took one breast in each hand. Her nipples were dark pink, with perhaps touch of brown and they were erect against the palms of his large, masculine hands. Connie was breathing deeply and looked up into his eyes. "Yes, be my barbarian." she said in a voice barely above a whisper.

Moving his hands up to her face he laced his fingers in her long hair, bent forward and kissed her passionately on the lips. She felt weakness in her knees and went with the feeling. Easing down, she dropped both knees to the carpet and was inches from his manhood which now stood at attention like a good soldier.

Tommy had not removed his fingers from her hair and let out a deep sigh, almost a growl as she took him into her warm, wet mouth. Looking down, the image of her performance caused his member ache and swell even more so than before. The muscles in his chest and shoulders tightened and he arched his back looking up at the ceiling. She was hungry, hungry to please him.

When he felt like he was going to explode, Tommy reached down, took her upper arms in his hands and pulled her to her feet. Without a word, he spun her around and guided her to the edge of the bed. Now she was on her hands and knees. Her beautiful, gym-toned bottom was facing him at the exact perfect height.

Looking back over her right shoulder, Connie pleaded, "Yes, barbarian, take me." Thrasher's right hand came down smartly on her ass cheek. Before she could protest, his left hand found her the opposite ass cheek. "Ow" she said, but did not protest. Now both of his hands gripped her waist. Her body was more than ready to receive him and his manhood entered and filled her. Unable to produce words, Connie gripped the sheets tightly and pulled them to her face. Her moans were deep and passionate. The sound inspired him all the more as he continued to thrust until there was no space between his pelvis and her sweet pink bottom.

Connie came up for air long enough to exclaim, "Oh, God, yes. Take me." Thrasher moved his right hand from her waist and found her hair. He took a firm hold of her hair and pulled her head up simultaneously as he thrusted. Now deep animal growls were coming from his throat. He was no longer a man, but a beast, an animal, the wild barbarian for which Connie begged.

Her waist and thighs began to quiver. The sweet scent of animal sex drifted up to his nose and the aroma pushed him over the edge. A deep growl, like that of a bear, escaped his throat. He was up on his toes. Every ounce of muscle in his strong legs tensed for the finish. His release came in waves. Connie's body shook and her breath came quickly.

Spent, his legs and knees weak, Tommy dropped down onto the bed beside her on his back. Slowly she squirmed over to him, wrapped an arm around him and nuzzled his chest with her face. After a long moment, with only the sounds of their breathing slowing and steadying, she spoke.

"Do you believe in Karma?" she asked. "Yes, I suppose in a way I do." he replied. "Well, Connie continued, "I believe that after all those years in a shitty marriage, Karma brought you here to me."

Tommy returned home from Connie's apartment around 10 p.m. He had stopped and topped off the truck's gas tank so that would be one less thing to do in the morning. Sarge was anxious to see him. He decided to forego the evening walk and simply let the lab out back to do his business in the yard.

After double checking his gear, Thrasher hit the rack and was sound asleep five minutes later.

SIX

The truck was loaded with Tommy's gear by 0730. Sarge was seated happily on the rear bench seat atop the seat cover specially designed for big, derpy dogs like him. Thrasher did not want to abuse the favor by showing up to Josh's house too early. Josh might not have minded a visitor at dawn, but Jennifer, his beautiful bride, might have been less than enthusiastic.

The silver Dodge 2500 eased into Mr. Josh Kimball's driveway a few minutes before 8 a.m. Sarge bounded from the truck and up to the front door, excited to be back. Josh and Reagan, the German Shepherd, were waiting at the door and welcomed them in.

"Coffee?" Kimball inquired holding his own cup aloft in the time honored gesture. "Yes, that'd be great. Thrasher replied and followed Josh to the kitchen. "Thanks again for keeping Sarge for me." Josh waved his hand to dismiss the thought. "You know he's welcome. Besides, the girls will tire both of them out so they sleep half the time." The girls were Josh's twin daughters; Jenna and Jewel, who had recently turned six years old. They had more energy than either the Shepherd or the Lab and the dogs would give up and go to sleep long before the girls did.

Jenny must have been getting the twins ready because none of them were in sight. Alone in the kitchen, Josh handed Tommy a cup of coffee and switched to business mode. "You have a contract, stateside?"

Thrasher felt a bit weird telling his contractor buddy that he was going to check in on a long lost love who might be in trouble. "It's more of a recon job than anything else. I'll be down around Vegas, Henderson specifically. I need a day, maybe two to figure out if it is something serious or not." Tommy filled in the blanks for his friend, not lying, but not needing to get into the "we were once in love" sad, pathetic story.

"Roger that. Josh replied in acknowledgement and continued "Henderson is a good six hours, you probably want to hit it." "Don't want to 'coffee and run' but yes." Thrasher set the cup down in the sink and turned to go.

"Hey there." a woman's voice called as she entered the room. "You going to run off without saying hello even?" Jenny entered the kitchen with the twins dressed for the day. Hugs were exchanged all around and the girls ran to find Sarge.

"I didn't want to bother you." Thrasher said to Jenny. "Bullcrap, you two were in here talking your secret squirrel shit, weren't you?" she said looking back and forth at both of them. When the girls were out of earshot Mrs. Kimball cussed like a sailor.

Both men laughed out loud. Tommy held up his hands, palms out in a surrender fashion. "I swear no secret squirrel shit, I'm just going out of town for a couple of days." "Whatever you say." Jenny responded heading toward the coffee pot herself.

Josh Kimball did not do much contracting anymore. He had officially retired from the US Army and had opened a training company in Salt Lake. Kimball held regular Concealed Carry permit classes for citizens. For a former Special Forces soldier, teaching mom and pop basic firearms safety and gun handling was a cake walk.

Although less frequent, Josh truly enjoyed putting on outdoor survival courses in the mountains surrounding the city. Kimball and one of his assistant instructors would take small groups, normally six to eight people, out into the the wilderness. Everyone was given a gear list and expected to hump all of it in a pack out to the woods. Josh would put on the courses for beginners in the late spring or summer. Winter courses were not for the faint of heart and Kimball relished the challenge of teaching serious winter survival skills to dedicated students.

The traffic on I-15 heading south away from Salt Lake City was not bad at all, the other direction was another story entirely. SLC was billed as a "small big city". Big enough to have all the modern amenities of a metropolis, but small enough to have a homey, friendly feel. That might have all been true, but traffic sucked during rush hour each morning and afternoon. Residents had to plan their travel around town accordingly.

After twenty minutes or so, Thrasher was able to set the cruise-control for 2 miles per hour over the posted speed limit. He knew that not even a State Trooper would pull you over for 2 miles over the limit, but he also felt like it helped him make good time. Tommy had the latest album from Solid Gold Cadillac downloaded onto his phone and played it through the truck radio.

He had nearly six hours left and as he drove he thought about his friend Josh. Thrasher had met Kimball on his first contract post-active duty. Kimball had only been dating Jenny back then. Tommy and Josh were both on a PSD (Protective Security Detail) contract for "State" (US State Department). Tommy was hired because of this skill and experience with a rifle as "Overwatch/Designated Marksman". When they met, Josh Kimball was technically still with the US Army Special Forces, but on reserve status. Kimball had completed numerous tours in Iraq and Afghanistan in his Army uniform, but for this assignment he was in the khaki pants and polo shirt uniform of the private military contractor.

Thrasher had processed out of the active-duty Marine Corps and into an Inactive Ready Reserve (IRR) status only one month before he touched down at Baghdad International Airport (BIAP) for his first contractor assignment. He had essentially been recruited to the contractor world while on deployment with the 2nd Marine Division. At the time his infantry company had been assigned the task of perimeter security and overwatch and worked closely with OGA contractors, all of whom were SOF guys. SOF was shorthand for Special Operation Forces; US Army Special Forces, US Navy Seals, Air Force Pararescue and Combat Controllers, and, of course, US Marine Corps MARSOC.

Josh Kimball, callsign "Gumball" for obvious reasons, was at BIAP to meet Tommy when he arrived. Along with Gumball was Buddy Kominski, callsign "Pyro" due to an unfortunate, but apparently infamous, incident with pyrotechnics. The two military contractors ushered Thrasher to a white Chevy Suburban and helped him get squared away.

Thrasher's original mission was supposed to be providing static overwatch with a rifle for the PSD team on the ground. In a perfect world, Tommy would be put in place to provide precision rifle fire to cover the team. He would be using a hyper-accurate M-16A4 rifle that the armorers had modified and outfitted with a match-barrel, tuned trigger, and variable power scope.

Though he did have a few actual overwatch assignments, reality dictated that the PSD team moved around with the protectee too frequently and too quickly for true overwatch to be practical. More often than not, Tommy found himself on the QRF (Quick Reaction Force).

Contract work proved to be much like being in the infantry. You went from a state of being bored out of you mind to hyper-alert or sheer adrenaline dump. Something that they never showed in the war movies was all down time and monotony that infantry soldiers experience between the excited panic of life and death combat.

When Tommy was a teenager, a friend's older sister, who was in college, told the two of them that "A truly intelligent person is never bored." She likely heard it from one of her professors and was laying her new found wisdom on her brother and his friend, but that phrase stuck with him. Thrasher tried his best never to say he was bored and to keep his mind active. During deployments with the 1st Battalion, 8th Marine Regiment, Thrasher read a great deal. There was always an empty MRE case filled with paperback books at the Charlie Company CP. You simply borrowed a book and tossed it back in the box when you had finished.

As a Military Contractor, there were long hours of "up time", where you were constantly on edge, scanning for threats, communicating with team members and keeping one step ahead of the enemy. There was also "down time". During this down time Gumball had introduced Tommy to barbell training.

Thrasher laughed out loud to himself when he thought of Josh's callsign, Gumball. Standard Operating Procedure (SOP) for all PSD contractors was to go by a callsign. This was primarily for radio communications, but callsigns stuck to everyone and real names, first or last were rarely used. Arriving on his first contract, Tommy had no callsign so it was up to Gumball, the Detail Leader (DL) to assign one to him. It was unusual for new guys to be allowed to make up their own callsign.

Gumball admitted that "Thrasher" would have been a badass callsign, but it was still his given name so that was a definite no go. During the first day, Josh Kimball, queried Tommy about his upbringing, where he was born, his childhood, where he had lived, etc.

When he was sixteen year old, Tommy's maternal grandfather had broken his leg in an accident on his dairy farm in Ohio. Tommy's parents sat him down and they all agreed that Grandpa Bill needed help quickly.

Sixteen year old Tommy Thrasher moved from his parents home in Michigan to his grandparents dairy farm located in the country near Mt. Vernon, Ohio. Tommy and his family visited the farm and stayed a week or so every summer so it was not foreign territory. It was agreed that Tommy would stay and help on the dairy farm until Grandpa Bill's leg was fully healed.

Tommy had met Beth Alexander in Mt. Vernon and had fallen in love. After their break up, he joined the Corps in Ohio, but that part was left out of the story he told Josh.

"Milkman!" Gumball had exclaimed as though the idea had jumped to the front of his brain. Because Thrasher had worked on a dairy farm, the DL had decided that Milkman was a perfect callsign. Thrasher had cringed and prayed that the sobriquet would not stick, but everyone on the team, Pyro especially, thought it was hilarious. Just like when he was a PFC fresh out of Infantry School in Charlie Company, 1/8, new guys needed to keep their mouths shut and their ears open. Milkman had stuck.

He hadn't been "Milkman" for a while. Thinking of it brought a grin to his face as he headed south on I-15 toward Henderson, Nevada.

There is no hunting like the hunting of man, and those who have hunted armed men long enough and liked it, never care for anything else thereafter.

Ernest Hemingway

SEVEN

The silver Dodge 2500 pulled up to the pump at a truck stop in St. George, Utah, near the Arizona border. Tommy wanted to top off the truck's fuel tank and give his legs a good stretch. Since leaving Gumball's house he had only pulled off the highway once to download the morning coffee. Thrasher bought a sliced deli meat sandwich and a cold bottle of water. He had plenty a water in the truck but it was not cold and he had already eaten a protein bar.

From his soft-sided briefcase, Tommy removed the burner phone. He had left it turned on deliberately in case there was a message from Beth with an update or telling him to forget it.
There were no new messages so he put the mobile phone away.

It was just after noon and Thrasher's plan was to get through Las Vegas before rush hour hit. Back behind the wheel he adjusted himself in the seat and gave his shoulders a good stretch. One of the downsides of road trips was the muscle stiffness that was sure to come. He felt a touch of soreness in his upper back and shoulders. During his last barbell training session he had worked the standing overhead press and he could certainly feel the results of the work he had done.

Entering the highway, Thrasher eased the truck back up to cruising speed. It was Josh that he owed a debt of gratitude for introducing him to barbell training. During that first contract in Iraq, Josh, as the DL, had worked some magic and acquired 500 pounds of Olympic plates, two barbells, a squat rack and vinyl covered bench. Tommy seemed to remember that all of the weight lifting equipment had come from the trade of two cases of Crown Royal (™) whiskey.

Josh was only about 5 foot 8 inches, but he was thick and as solid as a fire plug. It was he who showed young Thrasher how to execute a proper barbell squat, getting down, shoving his ass back and breaking parallel. "Most people cheat the squat, Gumball advised. "They squat about halfway down and go back up thinking that they accomplished something. That type of squat cheats your muscles and you'll never get real strength doing that."

Kimball had taught Tommy how to properly deadlift so he would not hurt his back. He also taught him the right way to overhead press and to bench press. Tommy had been bench pressing since high school football, but he never learned to set his back properly and do it right.

On Josh's advice, Tommy kept a notebook of his progress with the barbells. By the time he finished his first PSD contract he was demonstrably stronger all around. Between the barbells and the books he had to read, Milkman was never bored during his down time.

From the corner of his eye, Tommy spotted a black garbage bag on the right side of the highway. Without purposeful thought, he instantly checked his mirrors and moved to the left lane out of habit. His adrenaline had spiked ever so slightly. He again laughed out loud to himself after he has passed the discarded trash. There was little to no chance an IED (improvised explosive device) would have been placed along Interstate 15 on the Utah/Arizona border.

However, that is exactly what the insurgents and haj would do in Iraq. IED'd would be hidden in all manner of trash or refuse. Any object near the road was suspect. The enemy had even gone so far as to place bombs in dead animal carcasses; camels and goats.

As he made his way through the Virgin River Gorge in the northwest corner of Arizona, Tommy was struck by both the natural beauty of the landscape and the reality that is was a perfect stretch of highway for an ambush. He silently thanked God that there was nowhere like that in or around Baghdad. Afghanistan, however, was a different story altogether.

All along the twenty plus miles of I-15 through the Virgin River Gorge the highway wound like a snake. Ridges, hundreds of feet above the roadway, would give a perfect overlook for snipers or machine-gun emplacements. Vehicles on the highway had nowhere to escape. If you left the road you would drop down a ravine. Either that or you were boxed in against a sheer cliff wall.

Thrasher let his mind drift back to Baghdad and his first real action with the PSD team. The protectee, a State Department suit, most likely a CIA field agent, but that was never confirmed, was set for a meet up south of Baghdad outside of Rasheed. The incident had been debriefed from all angles, by everyone involved, so many times that it played back like a movie in Tommy's mind.

The mission had been simple enough from Tommy's perspective. He was a part of the QRF with two other men in "Blue Three"; Dallas, the Vehicle Commander and Fishstick, the driver. Thrasher was a JAFO. In contractor parlance JAFO stood for Just Another Fucking Observer. He would ride directly behind the driver so there would a shooter on the that side. If need be, the VC would shoot from the passenger side. Drivers don't shoot. Drivers drive.

For this op, the PSD team was attempting to keep a low profile, no obvious motorcade. A lead/scout vehicle "Blue Two" was out two clicks (Kilometers) ahead of the main vehicle "Blue One". Blue One included a driver, Ivy, Gumball was the DL/VC, and the protectee. The officially respectful callsign for the protectee, a mid-forties, caucasian male was "Papa One". His unofficial callsign was "Hairpiece". Papa One generally wore a tan baseball cap around the CP (Command Post) to cover the spreading bald spot atop his head.

However, once when a female State Department agent had visited, Papa One had showed up for a briefing wearing, not a ballcap but, a light brown hairpiece to match his remaining natural hair. Instantly he became "Hairpiece" to the team, at least when he was not in ear shot.

Ten minutes into the mission the Blue Two was hit by an IED. It had almost missed, but the explosion destroyed the right rear tire of their Toyota Land Rover and sent pieces of the adjacent quarter panel flying across the roadway. The back and right rear windows shattered into a thousand pieces. Pyro was in the front passenger seat and Montana, a former Army Ranger, was driving.

Every route had been preset with checkpoints and alternate escape routes. Pyro immediately radioed Blue One that they had been hit. Gumball turned to Ivy, to tell him to abort, but the driver already had the up-armored Chevy Suburban in a controlled "J-turn". They would return to the CP using alternate route Charlie.

Montana did his best to keep control of Blue Two, but they had been going nearly 60 mph when the IED hit them. The best he could do was execute a controlled crash approximately 300 meters from the explosion. Pyro radioed their situation; their vehicle was "bingo" (out of commision) and they had been hit and were stuck approximately 500 meters south of Checkpoint 2. The Toyota SUV had gone nose first in a shallow ditch, maybe a meter deep.

"Blue Three, Blue One," Gumball called over the radio. "Blue One, Go" The QRF was monitoring radio traffic, everyone had their game face on and the Blue Three Land Rover was loaded and idling at the compound gate.

Gumballs voice was calm and direct. "Blue Three, Blue One returning base route Charlie. Blue Two hit, 500 meters south of checkpoint 2, get to them ASAP." "Roger Blue One, Rolling".

Fishstick had the Land Rover up to 75 miles per hour less than a click out of the gate. Like any good driver, he studied road maps endlessly and had an exact mental picture of where the hit had taken place and very likely where Blue Two was stuck.

Dakota, the CP Communications agent in charge, immediately followed SOP and put in a call to "Big Army". The United States Army held overall command of Baghdad and the surrounding area.

Protocol stated that Big Army would be notified of any insurgent or enemy activity.

Montana and Pyro bailed out of their downed Toyota with their M4's in hand. Both were wearing a white "man dress" and red and white shemaghs. They wore full beards, per SOP, and to the casual observer they might pass as indigenous personnel. The loose traditional thaub, man dress, was actually very practical because it hid their body armor and kit. Both men had six M4 mags, two pistol mags for their Glock 17's and a portable radio on their armor plate carriers.

Diving down into the ditch for cover, Pyro yelled "Fuck, what's that stink!?" They both looked around and saw that the Land Rover had come to rest on a discarded goat carcass. The crash had mangled the animal corpses and the stink of the decomposing goat was horrible.

Then came the familiar zip and pop noise. Bullets began to hit on and around the exposed part of the crashed Toyota 4x4. Not surprisingly, the IED was "Go" signal for an ambush. Not wanting to miss a chance to kill some infidels, insurgents keyed in on the crashed vehicle with AK-47s.

Both PSD contractors were on the far side of the ambush with the Toyota between them and the incoming fire. "Stay low, we need to move." Pyro ordered and attempted to low crawl on hands and knees using the ditch for cover. While the man dresses were a good cover garment they made crawling next to impossible. Frustrated, the VC rolled onto his back, grabbed his radio and reported the situation.

"All Blue units, Blue Two, were taking small arms fire, repeat, we're under fire." "Copy Blue Two, Blue Three enroute, less than five mikes. Stay low." At that moment the staccato rhythm of a Soviet-designed PKM broke in, the Land Rover was being ripped to shreds by the 7.62 machine-gun. Pyro looked at Montana and stated what they both already knew. "Heads up, those fuckers are going to try to flank us."

"We've gotta be close. Fishstick called out loudly. "We just passed checkpoint 2." He slowed the Blue Three to 35 mph, they all knew haj was smart enough to know help would be coming for the downed vehicle. Without asking permission, Fishstick hit a right turn. "I know a back way in. There's an alley that the locals use as a day market. It'll be tight, but with all the fireworks, the locals should be running." "Okay, let's do it." Dallas agreed and keyed his radio, "Blue Two, Blue Three, we're coming in, going to backdoor the haj. Sit tight."

Just as Fishstick had said, they hit the marketplace alley and it was deserted. The locals heard the explosion and machine-gun fire and ran for cover.

There was just enough room for Blue Three Land Rover to squeeze between the vendors canopies and tables.

"There, right there. Fishstick pointed to the left. "That leads back to highway." He was pointing to an opening between two buildings, it was a walkway, not big enough for a vehicle. "I'd say less than a hundred meters." The vehicle windows were down and they could head sporadic AK fire and the PKM chopping away toward Blue Two. "Ok, stop." Dallas instructed.

"Milkman, you're with me. Fishstick, ease up close, but not too close, be ready to come in and get us when I call you." "Roger", the driver knew the drill. Dallas took off down the walkway with Milkman on his heels.

The machine-gun fire stopped. They're reloading Montana thought. Pyro looked left and right down the ditch. They had managed to get about forty yards from the shredded Toyota, but they had run out of ditch. If they kept moving they would be exposed from all sides. "Watch it." the VC said and a moment later saw two heads and then shoulders on the other side of the crashed 4x4. The insurgents were checking their work and looking for dead American bodies to film for propaganda.

Pryo rolled up on his side, shouldered his M4 and put the red aiming dot of his Aimpoint Comp M4 optic on the first body to come into view. "Pop, pop, pop," the M4 sent three 77 grain Mk262 bullets into Haj #1. He dropped. Haj #2 raised his AK to shoot over the vehicle wreck and caught two BTHP bullets to the upper chest. On cue, the Soviet machine-gun opened back up sending dirt and metal fragments everywhere.

Dallas and Milkman reached the end of the walkway and held at the corner. The machine-gun noise had stopped and then picked back up. Dallas did a quick peek right and then left. To the right, not fifty yards away was the PKM, one haj was on the gun and another was feeding him 7.62x54R belted ammunition.

To the left Dallas saw three haj spread out, hiding behind a couple of parked vehicles. Two had AK-47's and one man held an RPG-7 (Soviet-Era rocket launcher). All three were focusing intently on the highway in anticipation of the rescue team's arrival. The RPG was their welcoming gift for whomever showed up help out the first downed vehicle. The insurgent welcoming party was maybe forty to fifty yards away, opposite the machine-gun.

"Please tell me you have a grenade." Dallas said to Tommy. Thrasher smiled and showed his left hand. He had grabbed an M-67 fragmentation grenade from the Land Rover's backseat cupholder before they bailed out. Dallas held an olive drab green, baseball-sized explosive in his own hand.

Dallas keyed his portable radio, "All units, QRF in place. We're about to break the ambush. Standby." He didn't wait for a response. Looking to Tommy he said, "On three, throw it and hit the welcoming party. Shoot any haj with a gun. I'll take out the PK. Come back to me and we'll link up at the crash site. Tommy nodded in compliance.

Just like in bootcamp and then infantry school, Tommy thumbed off the grenade's safety clip, pulled the pin and cocked his right arm back. The RPG gunner would be his target. In a loud whisper Dallas said, "One, two, three." Both grenades flew threw the air. Their safety spoons coming off immediately and dancing in the air. With the noise of the PK machine-gun, none of the haj could hear the steel balls hit. Tommy's grenade dropped about ten feet from the RPG gunner and rolled. Dallas, his muscles pumped from all the barbell lifting, tossed his grenade hard enough that it hit and rolled up to the legs of the man feeding ammo to the machine-gun.

Within one second of each other, the twin grenades exploded. RRG man was hit with fragmentation. The jagged metal tore threw his body. He shook visibly, dropped the rocket-launcher and clutched his chest in shock. The man on his right was peppered with frag and jumped to his feet shocked at what had happened. Tommy wasted no time dropping him with two rounds. The other gunner reacted in the opposite fashion. He crouched down tightly and looked around. He had just about located Thrasher when a pair of 77 grain bullets punched his torso.

As it was designed to do, the grenade Dallas threw shredded the legs of the ammo man. He flipped over onto his back screaming and tried to access the damage. The proned out machine-gun operator had been hit as well. Pulling the Soviet death machine up he kept the trigger depressed and bullets flew skyward. Dallas fired at him rapidly. Five or six rounds tore into him from his groin to his neck. The ammo man, in shock, tried to scramble for the AK that was laying near him. Before he could reach it, Dallas popped him twice.

Dallas grabbed the radio. "Blue Two, gun is down, we're coming to you on foot. Repeat we're coming in on foot." "Got it, Blue Three." Pyro responded. "Fishstick we need you now."

Scanning for more insurgents, Thrasher and Dallas ran across the highway and covered the distance to the smoldering Land Rover in less than a minute. By the time the QRF men linked up with the Blue Two team, Fishstick arrived with the escape vehicle. All four climbed into the 4x4 rapidly and the driver didn't wait for the order to move out.

Success depends upon previous preparation, and without such preparation there is sure to be failure.

Confucius

EIGHT

The desert climate of Nevada reminded him of the desert country of Iraq. His memories of Iraq had kept his mind occupied for the trip through the Virgin River Gorge and on past Mesquite and Glendale, Nevada. Now the skyline of Las Vegas stretched out before him. At the intersection of Interstate 15 and 11, Tommy merged onto 11 South / East to skirt around "Sin City" and make the final approach to Henderson.

Traffic had been mild with no wrecks to contend with and Thrasher navigated into the Hilton Garden Inn parking lot before 2 pm. He was not at all surprised that the front desk host was very accommodating and able get him into a king room before the official check-in time of 3. Tommy had a Hilton Rewards membership and their staff tended to be top-notch, no matter what city he visited.

With his lodging taken care of, it was time to find a meeting place. Thrasher did not expect the threat level to be high, but he was also operating with very little intelligence at the moment. He wasn't going to take a chance that he might be set up or that Beth was being followed.

Not too far from the hotel, Tommy spotted a chain Taco joint. There was a strip mall parking lot adjacent that allowed full view of the Mexican fast food place. The spot was right off of E. Lake Mead

Parkway which would allow him rapid egress to the northeast away from the city or to the southwest back to Interstate 11.

The former Milkman decided that the Taco place would do and pulled into the lot for a close look inside. Like most fast food joints of that kind, there was a main dining area and a side area near the restrooms. The front was lit up well being almost 100 percent windows. As he expected, there was a fire exit out the back just past the restrooms.

Tommy ordered a burrito and bottle of water from the hispanic looking teenager at the counter, took it around the side and sat down to relax a bit. He was pleased that the fast food version of Mexican cuisine was actually rather tasty.

Back in his hotel room, Thrasher pulled out the burner phone. No messages from Beth. He composed a text.

In town. Meet at Taco Palace, 520 E. Lake Mead Pkwy.
Go inside, grab a coke, take a seat in a booth around the side.
4 p.m.

He hit the green send button, put his feet up on the corner of the small desk and waited. At 4 p.m. most fast food joints would be empty or close to it. There were only two booths on the side part of the restaurant so they should have some privacy.

Within five minutes the phone buzzed and light flashed.

Okay, I'll be there. See you soon.
Thank you again
Kitten

Tommy had an hour and a half before the meet up so he decided to hit the modest hotel fitness center. A half hour on the treadmill would help him work out the muscle stiffness from the drive.

Thrasher changed into workout clothes and running shoes. Before he left the room he picked up his personal phone and fired off a text to Josh.

Gumball
FYI - Arrived Henderson NV
Don't feed Sarge a bunch of hot dogs, you spoil him and make him fat
Milkman

Tommy hated running, but the short work out would get the oxygenated blood pumping to his brain and help him to think clearly and keep his mind sharp.

NINE

At 3:45 p.m. the silver Dodge truck was parked in the lot across from Taco Palace. Thrasher could see the surrounding parking lot, minus the rear of the building, and he had a clear view inside. The compact 8x binoculars sitting on the passenger seat aided his vision. He could pick out the faces of the people inside and out, no problem. At 3:51 he recognized the hispanic teen boy who served him earlier and watched him as he carried two bags of trash to the dumpster located at the edge of the lot. The boy tossed the trash in the big can and then immediately lit up a cigarette.

At 4:02 p.m. a tan Mercedes SUV entered the lot at pulled into a spot next to the building. The driver was a caucasian female, late twenties, early thirties with light brown, shoulder length hair, wearing large round sunglasses.

Elizabeth Alexander, at least that was her maiden name, stepped out of the SUV, looked around and walked inside. Tommy's pulse elevated as he laid eyes on her for the first time in over nine years. Thrasher watched her walk to the counter and begin to order.

About 45 seconds later, a black sedan with dark tinted windows pulled into the lot. Through his binos Tommy made it as a new model Chevy. The sedan looped around the parking lot once and then backed into a spot on the opposite side of the building from where Beth had parked.

After two minutes, no one had exited the black Chevy to go inside. The experienced operator knew that was not normal behavior. First of all, who backed into a spot at a taco joint? Then, after parking, why didn't anyone go inside? The front window of the Chevy was not tinted and Thrasher could make out the silhouettes of two people, likely men, in the front seat. They would have a clear view of the inside of the restaurant as well. Something definitely did not smell right.

"Who the fuck are you two?" Thrasher said out loud to himself. After two more minutes, there was no movement from the Chevy. Immediately he formulated a backup plan.

First a text message to Beth

I see you. When the police arrive, get in your car and drive immediately to Arnold's Grocery northeast on Lake Mead. Don't stop, don't look back. Park in the grocery lot and wait.
Acknowledge with Yes or No

Ten seconds later the word "YES" appeared on the screen.

Tommy dialed the direct dispatch number, not 9-1-1, to Henderson Police Department on the untraceable burner phone.

"Henderson Police Dispatch how can I help you." said the female dispatcher.

With a deliberately nervous voice, Tommy said, "I think someone is going to rob the Taco Palace at 520 Lake Mead. I saw two men with guns in a black Chevy sedan in the parking lot."

The dispatcher dutifully repeated what he had said. Tommy responded, "Yes, please hurry." "Thank you sir, can I have your name and phone number." she said with all the calmness of a seasoned dispatcher. "My name is Johnny White. Please hurry." Thrasher disconnected the call and waited.

Within two minutes Thrasher spotted the first cruiser and then the second. The street cops bracketed the black Chevy and exited, guns drawn yelled for the occupants to show their hands and get out.

Beth emerged from the fast food restaurant, walked rapidly to her SUV and was out of the lot in a quick minute. As he put the Dodge 2500 into drive and moved out to follow Beth, Thrasher took a long look at the scene. Two caucasian men, late thirties maybe early forties, were on their knees in the parking lot with hands on their heads.

Two minutes later, Tommy watched the Mercedes SUV come to a stop and park in the Arnold's Grocery lot. He was able pull up so his passenger door was next to Beth's driver's door. Rolling down the window he hollered, "Get in" At first she didn't see him, then she turned and made eye contact. He repeated, "Get in."

Thrasher reached across and popped open the passenger door. Beth Alexander grabbed her purse and scrambled inside climbing up into the truck seat.

"Close the door and don't say anything" he ordered. Beth obeyed quickly and Tommy maneuvered the truck out of the grocery store lot out onto Lake Mead Parkway. They took a right out of the lot and headed away from the Taco Palace scene. Thrasher watched his mirrors intently. He took a right on a side street, and then the next available right, and finally one more right until he was back to Lake Mead. No vehicle had remained behind the truck.

Two miles up the road was a casino. Thrasher turned into the large lot and parked next to a big black and tan RV on the outer edge of the parking area. He put the truck in park but left the motor running. Then he turned to look at Beth.

"First of all, hi, long time no see. Second of all, I don't suppose you have any idea who was following you?" Tommy could see in her eyes that she was in a state of shock. He'd seen it a hundred times before. She was trying to process all that was happening.

After a moment, she found her voice. "I, I, I'm not sure who was following me." Her breathing was rapid and she was trying to calm herself down. "Where is your phone?" he asked. She fished in her black leather purse and pulled it out to show him. "Turn it off." Tommy said. "What, why?" the words stumbled from her mouth. "Please, turn it off." he repeated in a more patient tone. She powered her iPhone down. Tommy reached into his nylon briefcase and produced a shiny, silver bag about 12x12 inches square. He gently took the phone from her hand and slipped it into the foil-colored bag. Once the bag was sealed he put it into his briefcase.

Beth had caught her breath. "What is that for?" "That is an RFID bag, he explained. "No radio signal can get in or out of it." She seemed a bit perplexed but did not protest.

"Thank you, thank you for coming." Beth managed in an excited tone. He could see that tears were welling up in her eyes. "I don't want to sit here for too long." Tommy explained and laid his right hand on her left leg. "Put your seatbelt on, we're going somewhere we can have a nice long talk."

TEN

Thrasher took the long way around to the Hilton Garden Inn. He parked the Dodge on the side of the hotel and used his room key to open the door to the back hallway. Tommy ushered Beth down the hallway avoiding the lobby to his room.

Once inside the room Thrasher showed Beth to one of the cushioned chairs, then he dropped his briefcase on the bed. Just for good measure, he opened it up and, after powering down the burner phone, slipped it into the RFID bag along with Beth's iPhone.

Thrasher opened a fresh bottle of water and handed it to her. "Take a drink." he said in a tone that was more a command than a suggestion. He took a seat in the chair opposite her. "Alright, I'm here now. No one knows where you are. Let's start from the beginning. What kind of trouble are you in and why do you think I can help you?"

Beth took a long drink from the water bottle. She had calmed down. At first she looked at the floor then she lifted her gaze to meet with his and she began.

After she began to talk she kept going for nearly twenty minutes. Thrasher sat silently and did not interrupt her at all, even when she paused to allow him to speak.

Beth explained that a year or so after their break up and his enlistment in the Marine Corps, she had met and then married Randall Ainsley. Ainsley majored in Business Management in college. Ainsley had jumped at an entry level management job as a nightshift floor manager at The Shining Star casino and hotel in Las Vegas. The Shining Star was a recent addition to the Las Vegas strip having been built on the site of an older casino by billionaire Vegas real estate developers. Randall turned out to be good with numbers and was subsequently promoted. He ended up in one of a few executive positions overseeing the books and cash receipts at the casino.

As she explained it, all was going well. Randall had worked his way up to a six figure salary and they bought a very nice house adjacent to a golf course in Henderson. They drove new cars, ate out all the time, socialized with other casino execs and were living the good life.

The two had no children. Beth said they had tried but then given up. Randall was too busy to worry about fertility tests and no one really wanted to raise their kids around Vegas anyway. He had also rationalized that they still had time for kids later if they wanted to have them.

Beth detailed their recreational or social drug use. They both smoked pot at parties and with friends.

"No big deal." she rationalized. Randall fell in love with cocaine. He often told Beth that it made him super-productive and never impacted his work. During one particular cocaine high, Ainsley had crashed a friend's 4x4 ATV down into a ravine. No broken bones resulted, but he ended up with serious muscle strains and lower back pain. A prescription for oxycodone helped with the muscle and back pain. Eighteen months later, Ainsley was still using the oxy on a regular basis.

Their primary physician had given Randall a single refill of the oxycodone. After the family doctor cut him off, he needed to look elsewhere to find a supply. As it turned out, buying oxy was not that difficult if you had cash money. That is when Randall met what Beth described as "those men".

During one of his oxy purchase transactions, Ainsley had been approached by a couple of men who explained in detail that they knew who he was and where he worked. They offered to protect him from being exposed as an illegal drug user.

Beth didn't need to tell Tommy that everyone who works for a casino in Nevada, particularly those who handle money, must cleared by the Nevada Gaming Commission. Any criminal activity, drug use, etc. was grounds for revocation of a Gaming Commission Registration. Without the State approval, it didn't matter how qualified Ainsley was at his job. He would be fired and no one in Vegas would or could hire him, at least not to work in a casino. They would go from a six figure income to zero overnight.

Beth had guessed that "those men" were involved in organized crime. She also said that Ainsley had been "working" with them for four or five months before he confessed any of it to her. They had had a big fight, as she explained it, some furniture had been broken. Randy, as she called him, stormed out of their house and stayed gone for two days.

When he returned home after the big fight, Randy had apologized, swore he'd get clean, and said he was going to tell "those men" he was through. According to Beth's timeline that was three or four months earlier. She claimed that not much had changed. Randy was still using. He wouldn't tell Beth anymore about "those men" and claimed that it was "all under control".

Thrasher let it all sink in for a bit. He was not a cop or an investigator, he was a fighter, a killer perhaps, but he had also learned quite a lot while working as a bodyguard and PSD agent. There were definitely some big pieces of the puzzle missing. Sure her husband was a drug user, and probably dirty from his association with what had to be organized crime figures. But why the hell was she scared? A good divorce lawyer could help her cut ties with the douche and she'd be free to move on with her life.

He also knew one spouse could not be compelled to testify against the other.

If she was telling the truth, she could claim ignorance of the illegal activity, minus prescription and illegal drug use. Certainly an admission of smoking pot would not ruin her life forever. She was holding back. Thrasher was sure of it.

Tommy took a deliberate deep breath and spoke. "It sounds to me like you need a good divorce attorney. I saw billboards for at least a dozen on the highway coming into town. Grab your purse, I'll give you your phone and take you back to your car. It's been nice catching up." He then got up from his chair, turned his back to her and walked over to the bed to retrieve her phone from the briefcase.

"What, just like that?" she stammered after a second. He turned and looked her directly in the eyes. "Yes, just like that. You just told me a story of shitty marriage to a selfish asshole. I'm not a marriage counselor or divorce lawyer. Get up. Let's go."

Beth Alexander/Ainsley didn't move from her seat. She broke eye contact and looked down at the floor. "Look at me." Thrasher said, it was not a suggestion. She raised her head, tears were welling up again. "Turn off the tears. You tell me everything, not just the parts you want me to hear or we're headed out the door and I'm going back to my life."

"Okay, okay. Please don't turn me away" she pleaded. Tommy returned to his seat. His play had seemed to work. "Alright. he said, "Why did you send me that email? Don't tell me it was because your husband is hooked on Oxy."

ELEVEN

Tommy was up at 6 a.m. It was a habit to be up at sunrise, but today there was no Sarge to take for a walk. Beth was still asleep in the king sized bed next to him. Without waking her Thrasher dressed and headed to the breakfast cafe in the main lobby of the hotel. Hilton's always had a restaurant or cafe and that was one of the perks he appreciated.

Returning to the room with two hot coffees and two ham, egg, and cheese breakfast croissants, Tommy found Beth laying in the bed but now she was awake. "Here you go, breakfast is served." he said setting the coffee and food down on the small table between the two cushioned chairs.

Beth thanked him and crawled out from between the covers. She was wearing one of his t-shirts and panties. He caught a glimpse of her smooth, shapely legs, her red painted toes, and felt that old feeling stirring inside.

They ate and sipped coffee in silence. Tommy was contemplating all that she had told him last evening before. He was also honestly stumped, he had no idea what move he should make. He was trying to formulate some kind of plan when he drifted off to sleep sometime after 11 p.m.

Beth had spilled the remainder of the story. She had suggested months earlier to Randy that he go to the police, get a good attorney, and then check into drug rehab. Ainsley had rejected the idea, told her that the police would not help and that they'd be ruined.

She also confessed that for nearly a year, rather than using her using a credit or bank card to pay for what she needed around the house, Randy gave her cash. It would be better "for their taxes" if she just paid cash Randy told her. He would give her cash, five hundred to a thousand dollars at a time. She claimed that she protested at first, but then she stopped asking questions and simply took the cash.

Beth also admitted that she and Randy hadn't slept together in many months. He would stay in town (Vegas) until late at night or sometimes he'd text and say it was "too late" to drive home, he'd just grab a bed at the casino. She strongly suspected that he was "fucking some whore" or several from the casino. She admitted that she'd been upset about it at first but then became indifferent.

When he was at home, Randy always seemed distracted or nervous. He got angry over the stupidest little things and lashed out. She decided that the more time he was gone at work or whatever, the better.

It took some prodding, but Beth confessed that she had begun an affair, a casual one she assured him, with one of the professional trainers at the fitness center where she took yoga classes. After the first encounter she told herself it was a one time thing, but then it happened again and again. She knew Randy would be in Vegas all day and maybe not even come home at all. She had allowed Carlos, the trainer, to come to her house for casual relations.

The day before she sent Tommy the email, she had come home alone from shopping. She'd bought some new clothes and shoes, cash payment, of course. On her doorstep was a large manila envelope. In black marker on the outside was written, *Don't Fuck Up a Good Thing.*

Inside of the envelope were a half dozen 8x10 color prints. There were pictures of her going in and out of the yoga class, and two very clear shots of Carlos entering through the front door of her house with Beth standing there holding it open and one of Carlos leaving. Beth had convinced Tommy that the envelope scared the shit out of her. She realized she was being watched. She claimed she did not know by whom.

Beth rationalized that if she went to the police or a divorce attorney now, she didn't know what those men would do. Would they hurt Randy? Would they hurt her? That was when she sent the email.

She lied to Carlos and told him that her husband was suspicious and that they needed to "cool off" and "take a break". Beth said that she was "being careful" that she "looked around a lot". He didn't have to explain that she was not very good at spotting a tail. That would be hurtful.

They had decided that since Arnold's Grocery was a 24 Hour a day store that her SUV would not likely be towed. Also, since Tommy was convinced that is was very likely her house was being watched, it was best for her to stay at the hotel, at least for the night.

Thrasher still did not know what he was up against. The men following her were obviously skilled at surveillance. He was not sure at all how long they'd been watching her or of what they were truly capable. Did they have the sophistication to track her with her iPhone. He was glad he'd dump it in the RFID bag. Also, he did not know to what level Randy had immersed himself with the gangsters. Was this a stern warning or leg breaking situation or a shallow grave in the desert situation?

Tommy also tried to weigh her criminal culpability in his mind. The cash she was using was most certainly off the books and, more likely than not, dirty. The courts might not be able to make her testify against Randy, but she might end up charged with something criminal. If she ran to an attorney or tried to cut a deal with the cops, would "those men" ever allow her to open her mouth? It was most definitely a shit sandwich.

Thrasher also had to search his soul. Why should he let himself get mixed up in this? Afterall, she was a long ago love affair that ended badly. Did he owe her? The disciplined war-veteran in him was angry with his sentimental side for being soft. Logic said he should drive her straight to the police and tell her to beg for mercy and get some kind of witness protection. But, did it even work that way? The police might take a statement and send her home. Then what? Shit.

Also, there was that douchebag, Randy. Had he returned home to find her missing? How would he react? Surely he'd tried to text or call her. There was no way that Tommy was going to power up the iPhone to find out. Randy might have already figured out she was fucking the yoga guy and decided that fair was fair. Or, was he freaking out and reporting her as a missing person? Thrasher decided to deal with what he could control and not to worry about what he could not control. He could not control what Randall Ainsley did or did not do. Fuck that douche, anyway.

He was certain about one thing, there was no way Beth could simply drive home and try to resume a "normal life". Normal life was out of the question, at least for the foreseeable future.

TWELVE

Randy Ainsley had not returned home the previous night. As he had dozens of time before, Randy fired off a simple text to his wife at five minutes past 8 pm.

Working late, too late to drive home. I'll get a room at The Star. Goodnight

Beth used to respond or even ask questions about his overnight Vegas stays, but lately she rarely responded. In Randy's mind he had fulfilled his obligation to let her know he had not been killed in a car crash, so she need not wait up for him.

Ainsley had indeed worked late, he did not leave his office on the second floor of The Shining Star until almost 7pm. It was also true that he did not feel like driving home. Beth would either ignore him or start in again on him about "getting clean". Neither option had much appeal. Instead he had sent a text much earlier to Crystal.

Up for some fun tonight? Meet me in my room after your shift.

Crystal Day had come to Las Vegas at age twenty with the dream of dancing in a big Vegas show. She had been the best dancer in her performing arts class, at least that is what her instructor had confided to her during post-coital bliss.

After one too many rejections from casting directors, Crystal decided she loved the excitement of Las Vegas and if she could not be a dancer in Sin City, she would stay and enjoy the life. The Shining Star was hiring cocktail servers and she found that the cash tips were generous, particularly when the gamblers at the tables noticed her ample cleavage.

Randy took notice of her immediately, and he particularly appreciated her firm and fit dancers' body. Banging cocktail waitresses was taboo for casino executives and he had warned Crystal to keep their relationship on the down low.

Second shift, from 3 to 11 pm was the good money for cocktail servers. Crystal could finish her shift, change from her revealing black "hostess" uniform into some street clothes, and meet Randy in room 2022, by 11:30 at the latest.

The 20th floor had several rooms that were reserved for high rollers. The executives could sign them out for the night as a perk if they had not been reserved. Room 2022 was on the far end of the hallway and it overlooked the backside, toward I-15, not the strip. Therefore, few high rollers rarely, if ever, requested it. Room 2022 had become Randy Ainsley's love bungaloo.

Ainsley knew Crystal would come. She loved the excitement of banging in a high roller suite. The room had a jacuzzi tub, king sized bed, and Randy always had coke. She was young, fit and wild in the sack. Randy had to be careful to balance the oxy and the coke so his performance would not be affected.

Ainsley knew Crystal would head to the room promptly after her shift ended at 11, so he had some time to kill. Randy walked the floor of the casino like a cock rooster. The floor was active, lots of people at the tables and the slot machines. He spotted a new hostess, one he had not seen before. She had long, dark hair and pale skin. Her bosoms were barely contained by the skimpy black outfit. Randy made a note to himself to find the floor manager and inquire about the new girl.

He treated himself to a steak and a couple glasses of Jim Beam at The Star's steakhouse. When the check came Ainsley charged it to his manager's card. He didn't have a bill smaller than a twenty so he told himself that he would make it up to the server the next time he ate there.

On the third floor of the parking garage he met his coke guy for the normally scheduled exchange. Randy walked past a fire engine red Ford Mustang, stuck his hand into the lowered passenger side window. A red and white $100 table chip from his palm and was replaced by a baggie of coke, the good shit, not street junk. The entire transaction took no more than 30 seconds. Ainsley smiled as he walked back inside. *Membership has its benefits* he thought to himself. Thanks to his association with connected people, Randy always had the good shit. No real cash was needed. The poker chip set up had been put in place months before.

All set with party favors, Ainsley made his way to the hotel tower elevator. It was nearly 10:30 as he fished the card key for 2022 out of his front pocket. All the way up his mind was consumed with carnal thoughts about Crystal's hard firm body and having her legs wrapped around his waist. He inserted the key into the slot, the light on the door lock showed green and Randy turned the knob to open it. Then a bright light flashed in his eyes and the world went dark.

The first impulse Randall Ainsley felt was the aching pain at the base of his skull. He opened his eyes and had to force himself to focus. His vision was blurry, but then it cleared and there were two very large men standing in front of him one black and one white. Randy shook his head in an attempt to clear it and found some righteous indignation.

"What the fuck!" he blurted and attempted to get up from one of the suite's super comfortable lounge chairs. The black one landed a meaty closed fist directly to Randy's gut. The air from his lungs burst forward with loud grunt and he felt cold panic that he might puke on the expensive rug.

"What the fuck is right. The white one said. "Where the fuck is your wife?" Ainsley did not attempt to stand up again. He stared at the white one, not sure he understood the question. The black one raised a clenched fist to hit him again. "Stop, stop!" Randy pleaded. The black one held the punch back. "I don't know where she is. She should be at home."

"Well, she is not at home, and either you or she thought it would be funny to sic the cops on our people." The white one paused looking for some sense of recognition. Randy was indeed confused, 'sic the cops on our people'? He had no idea what the thug was talking about.

Taking his silence as guilt, white thug nodded at black thug. This time Randy received an open palm smack to the head. The bright lights reappeared but he did not lose consciousness.

Ainsley threw his hands up to ward off future blows and sunk back into the chair as far as he could get. "I swear to you I don't know what the hell you are talking about. I've been here working all day. I saw Beth when I left the house at 6:30 this morning. I don't know where the fuck she is or what she is doing."

The white one spoke to Randy like he was speaking to a child. "Okay, well either you or she, or the two of you together, thought it would be funny to put the cops on our people down in Henderson earlier today. What Jimmy and I are here to find out is what the fuck is going on in your head or her head. You better come up with some answers before you end up pissing blood."

Ainsley was trying desperately to make sense of the situation and come up with words that would prevent further pain. "So, you guys were following her?" he said out loud as the thought entered his head. Black and White exchanged glances then looked at him in unison.

Fearing the beating to come, Ainsley blurted out, "Look, she's cool. She takes the cash I give her and doesn't ask questions. She's shut up about the cops, I told your boss. Everything is cool."

"Hey asshole, Jimmy, the black one, spoke for the first time, "Do you think we'd be standing here if everything was 'cool'? Do we look like guys that would waste our time with you if everything was 'cool'?" Ainsley didn't dare answer the rhetorical question. He had learned that much in the last five minutes.

The white thug, still unnamed, took over. "Get on your fucking phone and call your cunt wife, right now." Randy struggled to remain in the chair while digging his phone from his left front pocket. He hit the speed dial button and it went directly to her voicemail. "Voicemail" he said meekly. "Bullshit dial again." Randy hit redial and White Thug snatched the phone from his hand and pressed the speaker button. Beth Alexander/Ainsley's voice came on immediately asking the caller to leave a message. Beth's phone was obviously turned off. The frustrated thug tossed the phone across the room.

"Okay asshole, White Thug said, "I suppose that we need to come up with a plan 'B'." Randall Ainsley immediately prayed that plan 'B' did not involve him pissing blood.

Courage is resistance to fear, mastery of fear, not absence of fear.

Mark Twain

THIRTEEN

"How much cash can you get your hands on?" Tommy Thrasher said to Beth who was freshly showered and redressed in the clothes she had on the day before. It was nearly noon and he needed to figure out what to do. They could not just hold up in the hotel and wait for the cavalry to arrive.

"I'm not sure how much it is, but Randy keeps a lot of cash in a safe at home. I probably have between $400 and $500 there in my purse."

"Can you get into that safe? Thrasher continued without waiting for an answer. "The way I see it you have a couple of options. A: you find a good lawyer, spill your story to him or her. They arrange a meeting with the local cops and try to work some kind of immunity deal with the local D.A. Maybe they put you in some kind of witness protection, maybe they don't and tell you that you are on your own. B: you try to go back to your life as normal, keep taking the cash from your husband and hope that he gets clean and it all works out." "Is there a third option?" she asked.

"Yes, option C is that you grab as much cash as you can get your hands on, pack whatever you can in a couple of suitcases and get the hell away from here. The guys in the black Chey at Taco Palace are certainly the ones who have been following you and took the pictures that mysteriously ended up on your doorstep. They know what you drive, where you live and shop. They also know that you've been banging the yoga guy on side." That last remark earned Tommy a scowl from Beth.

Thrasher dismissed her frown and continued. "You're a grown woman, you have to make a choice. I can't make it for you." "I've never tried to get into the safe. I never needed to, but I am pretty sure that I know the combination. Randy will lose his shit if I take the money he's been stashing."

Tommy could sense that she was still holding on to the hope that somehow she could go back to the way things used to be. Why else would she be worried about how her husband reacted to the missing money? Thrasher was not so naive as to believe the off-the-books cash Randall Ainsley had been giving her and stashing was clean money. Whatever he was doing for "those men" was most definitely dirty. He also had a strong suspicion that his play with the Henderson P.D. would not scare off the bad men. They might be more cautious in the future, but her husband was apparently in pretty deep with criminals, not street hoods. Street hoods did not conduct surveillance and tail people.

"Look, I know it is a lot to process. Tommy used a consoling tone. "But be honest, when you sent me that email you knew things were getting bad. Do you really believe that your husband is going have a 'Come to Jesus' moment, get clean and cut ties with whoever it is that he is working with?"

Beth looked at the floor of the Hilton Inn hotel room for a long moment, then spoke. "It's just, it's just that we've been together for so many years. Things haven't always been bad with Randy. He's been good to me. We made a life out here." Beth Alexander/Ainsley sounded just like most every abused woman of which Thrasher ever heard or encountered. She held out hope that her husband would change and that everything would go back to the way it was. Tommy's life experience told him that her hope was a false hope. That kind of miracle change almost never happened, but her female brain was desperately holding on to that exact thought. He decided to shift gears at take smaller steps.

"Is there anything in your SUV that you cannot live without?"

You have enemies? Good. That means you've stood up for something, sometime in your life.

Winston Churchill

FOURTEEN

Carlos Jimenez had a number of regular clients. Normally, he did one or two morning sessions for housewives that didn't have to work and then a couple in the evening for those clients who came in after they left work. Jimenez was a fit, muscular 28 year old man. Carlos' parents emigrated from Mexico when he was only 3 years old. He had dark hair, brown eyes, and despite his hispanic background he spoke English like he had been born in the United States, not the broken English of a gardener or dayworker.

Dozens of bored housewives filled his yoga classes at Henderson Fitness and Spa. It was not difficult to convince a select few, who were spending their husbands' money, to become his personal clients for one to one training sessions. Carlos had worked himself into a Win/Win situation at the spa. He charged the housewives $75 an hour for personal training and as often as not, he would allow himself to be seduced by them. He got paid to keep them in shape and then he took advantage of their fit bodies in the bedroom. Currently he was bedding three bored housewives whose husbands spent too much time in the office and not enough time keeping them happy.

It was common for the husbands to eventually get suspicious or jealous of all the time their wives were spending at the spa or in personal training.

The women would quit all together if their men pulled the plug on the money or they'd tell him that they just wanted the fitness training and nothing else.

The money was good and he was doing well enough that he could be selective as to whom he took on as personal clients. Things had gotten freaky too. One of his clients wanted sex only after a hard training session, when she was all worked up and sweaty. He had obliged her.

Another woman had him make a housecall. When he arrived, her husband was there, but she quickly explained that is was all cool. Her husband wanted only to watch. His first instinct was to head out the door, but he was assured that he would be well compensated for his time. It didn't hurt that she was naked in only high heels when he arrived.

As agreed, the husband sat in a comfortable chair and watched silently as he serviced the fit and firm housewife with great vigor. Afterward, he found that he was not only comfortable with it, but it rather turned him on. He was a young, virile buck who took the woman while her middle-aged husband sat and watched. He was a stallion he thought, *el semental!*

One of his recent conquests had decided to cool it off. She claimed that her husband was getting suspicious. Though he was disappointed, she was extremely enthusiastic in the bedroom, he knew he would replace her soon enough.

As he walked across the Henderson Spa parking lot to his green Jeep Wrangler, Carlos thought about the redhead who had just recently started taking the group yoga classes. She seemed eager and never flinched when he put his hands on her to help her get into position. So engrossed were his thoughts of the redhead that he didn't see the man approaching from behind.

Jimenez was shocked from his daydream when a muscular hand grabbed his arm. He spun to face the attacker and felt a hard steel object jab into his guts. On cue a black four door sedan pulled up. "Shut your mouth and get in." said a large black man that Carlos instantly realized had a pistol pressed to his ribs.

The rear door popped open and Jimenez allowed himself to be shoved into the rear seat. Inside the car was another man, a large white one in the back seat and a driver. Carlos was wedged in between the two men in the rear seat. "Don't panic, we aren't going to kill you. said the white one. "But we do need to have a talk."

As the car took off down the street, Jimenez began to sweat profusely. Which womans' husband had found out? The pistol was still poking his ribs. The white man pulled out an 8x10 color photo and held it up to his face.

Carlos felt the urge to vomit as he recognized himself from the rear standing in the doorway of Beth Ainsley's house. "Look, she came onto me." he blurted out. "Shut up and listen" the large white man said. Jimenez obeyed and was silent. "You've been fucking this woman for a while and I really don't care. But, she is missing and we need to find her."

Jimenez mind raced. 'What does he mean, missing? Did they think he had something to do with that?' "I haven't seen her in a couple of days. I didn't do anything to her. I swear." "No one said you did, white thug said. "Pull out your phone and send her a text. Tell her you miss her."

Carlos found his phone and did as he was told. His fingers were trembling, but he managed to send at text

Hey, how are you? I miss you. Can I see you again?

While they waited for a reply, the man grilled Jimenez. Where did they go together? Coffee house? Restaurant? Did they also go to a hotel or his house for sex?

Gino, the white thug, had most of the answers to the questions he was asking the hispanic man. The private investigators that they employed were, with one recent exception, very good at their job. He had read the P.I. reports on the Ainsley woman. Gino's experience with interrogation was that it was always good to ask the subject questions to which you already had the answers to test their truthfulness.

After nearly thirty minutes of driving, no reply had appeared on Carlos' phone that was now in the hands of the big white man. Jimenez' bladder was aching and he thought he might piss on himself.

"Alright, this will do" the interrogator said to the driver. The sedan pulled into a strip mall parking lot and stopped. The interrogator turned and looked Carlos in the face. His expression was deadly serious and the yoga instructor felt cold sweat dripping down his back. "Do you suppose you'll be a very good personal trainer with a broken spine?", he asked rhetorically.

Jimenez allowed the threat to sink in. He didn't speak but shook his head slightly. The thug held up a small white piece of paper in front of Carlos' face, there were only ten digits written on it. "If and when she contacts you, text this number immediately." After a moment of hesitation, Carlos meekly took the piece of paper from the thug's hand. "You can forget our faces and forget this ride ever happened.

But don't you forget to text the second she contacts you."

The large black man opened his door, pulled Jimenez out of the back seat and forced him roughly out into the parking lot. "Don't forget" the black one said. He climbed back into the sedan, and it pulled away. At that moment Carlos' bladder gave up the fight and let go.

FIFTEEN

The Silver Dodge 2500 was parked about 200 yards away from Beth's SUV. Tommy sat behind the wheel with binoculars in hand. He scanned every vehicle that seemed like it might have a view of her tan Mercedes. After approximately forty-five minutes, Beth was getting impatient, Thrasher was satisfied that the likelihood that Beth's vehicle was being watched by anyone in the lot was slim at best.

The current Mrs. Randall Ainsley insisted that she needed her car. After further discussion with Tommy, Beth had stated that she would take all the cash she could get her hands on and her Mercedes SUV and leave Randy. She had not committed a crime, she said, so there was no reason for the police to be looking for her car. Beth also rationalized, and Tommy tended to agree, that once she was far away from Las Vegas those men would have no reason to follow her or even look for her. She would go to a city where no one would look for her, give Randy a few months to get cleaned up, and then, if she felt comfortable, she would contact him.

Thrasher did some rationalizing of his own. He was not married or in any type of relationship with Beth. He could only give her advice. It was up to her to take it or not. If he helped her get safely away from her crooked, drug-addicted husband, that would be a positive end to the Henderson, Nevada adventure. Afterall, he had a life to get back to, he could not bodyguard her indefinitely.

Beth had given Tommy the address to her house and the two had mapped out the route that she would take back home. It was still early afternoon, not quite five p.m. According to Beth, when he did come home, Randy never arrived before seven. They had stopped at a big box store and purchased another "pay as you go" mobile phone; a burner. Tommy set up the phone, put his burner number on speed dial and gave it to Beth. As a precaution, he advised her to keep her personal phone turned off, but he gave it back to her.

The plan was simple, or so Thrasher thought. Beth would drive the SUV directly to her house with Tommy tailing at a good distance. If Tommy spotted a new tail on her he would call. She would drive immediately to the casino where they had stopped the day before, park, and walk directly through the front door. Tommy would pull to the far side by the shuttle entrance and wait for her. Beth had gambled there many times and she knew the layout well.

"Alright, Tommy said "Let's get going. Any questions?" "No, we've gone over it ten times, I think I've got it." Beth playfully mocked Thrasher's thoroughness. She opened the door and stepped out. Thrasher anxiously watched as she closed the distance. Beth reached the Mercedes without incident. She had unlocked it with a remote from a distance and quickly climbed inside. Within two minutes she was pulling out of the lot. "Not too close." Thrasher reminded himself and he moved out behind her.

Tommy kept a good distance, nearly a kilometer or more by his estimation. If someone was going to pull in and tail her he needed to be far enough back to catch it. Once he caught a red light, but he was able to catch up shortly. He had advised Beth to drive about five miles below the speed limit.

It was only about a ten minute drive to the subdivision where Randy and Beth lived. When they pulled onto the side street off of the main road Thrasher felt a sense of relief. All had gone well. He had previously viewed her house and the surrounding neighborhood with an overhead GPS map on his phone. She would pull into her driveway up to the house and he would drive past, turn around and wait near a service road that led to the nearby golf course. Most of the high end housing in Henderson was adjacent to golf courses. There was no way Thrasher wanted to risk getting blocked in her driveway by a surprise guest.

By his estimation from the street map, as he turned into the subdivision Beth would be entering her driveway. The burner phone in the console rang and gave Tommy a slight surprise, he never kept the ringer turned on, but for this occasion he did.

Thrasher grabbed up the phone. There was only one person who would be calling. "Randy's home. His car is in the drive." Beth said. "Turn around and leave." Tommy immediately instructed. "I have to face him. I owe him at least that much" she replied. "Bad idea. Stick to the plan." Thrasher felt his guts start to move. It was that feeling he had so many times before. "I'll be alright. You sit tight and I'll call you." Beth said and then hung up the phone. She had pulled into her driveway next to a white Nissan GT-R sports car. Thrasher did his best to drive "casually" past her house. He watched Beth get out and walk to the front door.

A quarter mile down the street Thrasher found the golf course service road and turned the truck around so it was backed in. He hope that no nosey neighbors would call and report a suspicious vehicle. The good news was that he was driving a truck, a work vehicle, unlike all the others he saw on the street. With any luck the locals would assume his truck was part of the golf course work crew.

Tommy checked the time. It was 5:21 p.m. How long should he give her? How long before he should worry?

Battle is the most magnificent competition in which a human being can indulge. It brings out all that is best; it removes all that is base. All men are afraid in battle. The coward is the one who lets his fear overcome his sense of duty. Duty is the essence of manhood.

General George S. Patton

SIXTEEN

The sun was starting to drop in the west and the commuters were beginning to return home. Thrasher estimated that most of the homes in the subdivision were in the $500,000 to $1,000,000 price range. You didn't make that kind of money as the day shift manager for a grocery store in Henderson. Thrasher surmised that most of the residents of the neighborhood commuted into Las Vegas each day to work.

Tommy watched the SUV's and cars drive past. Some held a single male occupant, others a mom with kids. Halfway down the street he saw an SUV pull into the drive and discharge a young man and likely his sister in white Karate uniforms with the matching colored belts. The mom was carrying large bags of take out from on of the local restaurants.

The thought of a "Homestyle to Go" meal; mashed potatoes and gravy, chicken, maybe roast beef, made Thrashers stomach churn a bit. He looked at his wristwatch, it was 5:49 p.m. and he hadn't eaten since they left the hotel earlier that day.

Though he had kept his mind busy with observation of the comings and going of the neighborhood, Thrasher was starting to become more anxious. He had rationalized to himself that Beth would likely get into an argument with her husband. She said he had never physically assaulted her, but furniture had been broken. It was reasonable to expect that it would take at least 30 minutes or so for the emotions to come out and then to settle back down, maybe a bit longer.

What would she tell Randy? During the detailed planning phase they had not covered the possibility that Beth would have to confront her husband. Thrasher kicked himself mentally for making that mistake. Would Beth spill her guts completely? Would she tell him she was taking her money and leaving him? If she did, would Randy try to physically stop her? Or, would she make up a cover story and try to smooth it over?

As experienced as he was dealing with deadly threats and enemies overseas, Tommy felt like an amatuer now dealing with all of this marriage drama. Being a Marine infantryman was much simpler and straight-forward; make a plan, locate the enemy, kill the enemy by fire and maneuver. There was a brutal honesty to combat, that is, real genuine combat. Combat was barbaric, horrific, and initially terrifying to those new to it, but there was also a sort of cosmic honesty. Thrasher hated the political correctness, half-truths, and drama that he permeated the civilian world. A friend had said to him, "You spend more time with your dog than with other people." That friend was partially right. Sarge was honest and loyal and there was no drama there.

Thrasher made the decision that he would give Beth until 6 p.m. to call and then he would go check on her. He lamented that he could not see her driveway entrance from his hiding spot. He had considered just parking on the street, but that might attract nosey neighbors and a visit from Henderson PD. Every neighborhood had at least one Gladys Kravitz, sometimes more. His out of state plates might raise eyebrows of the noisy homebodies.

At 6:01 p.m. the sun had reached the peaks of the mountains west of Las Vegas. Long shadows were cast on the Henderson subdivision. While it was not yet dark, it would be soon enough. Thrasher formulated a plan. He would slip out of the truck and use the edge of the golf course to make his way to the back of Beth's house. From the aerial map he knew there were four houses between the service road and the Ainsley home. Palm trees and decorative shrubbery lined the course and acted as a barrier between the fairways and the backyards of the homes that sat adjacent to it.

It seemed reasonable to Thrasher that he could skirt the edge of the course, use the trees and foliage for cover and reach the stonewall that surrounded the backyard of the Ainsley home undetected. From the back seat of the truck Tommy grabbed a plain black pullover, hooded sweatshirt. He was wearing dark gray, loose fitting pants and black lace-up leather boots. He knew his white face and hands would give him away in the shadows so from under the rear seat he retrieved his black shooting gloves. There were insulated cold weather gloves as well as a fleece balaclava pullover hood. He would not need the hood for warmth, but it would cover up his white skin as he navigated the shadows.

Thrasher pocketed the burner phone after he turned off the ringer. He would take the compact binoculars with him. The large hand pocket on the front of the sweatshirt would conceal the binos so he would not appear so much like a pervert voyeur. He would not cover his face until he was close to the target. On his body was his everyday gear; pistol, spare mag, folding knife, flashlight, and compact trauma kit.

The truck door was closed slowly and gently and Tommy manually locked it instead of using the remote which always activated a short horn beep. Thrasher secured the truck key in a secure zipper pocket in his pants. It was 6:12 p.m. when he slipped quietly behind the truck and began to maneuver along the edge of the fairway masked by palm trees, palmetto bushes and other shrubbery.

Thrasher's plan was to get to the backyard wall of Beth's house and find a vantage point to see inside. He needed to relieve his anxiety and see her safe and sound inside the house, doing whatever. Maybe, just maybe, she would be having a civil heart to heart with her husband. Tommy reminded himself that minus any real intelligence, he had to assume she was merely hashing it out with the old man.

Aside from an armadillo that had come noisily crashing out of the palmetto bushes, scaring the shit out of Tommy for a second or two, the movement to the rear of the Ainsley home had been uneventful and took only about five minutes or so.

Thrasher knew from the overhead photos that there was a kidney shaped pool in the backyard, as well as a maintenance shed in the corner of the property. Thrasher used a cluster of palm trees to hide his silhouette and was grateful for the coming darkness. He could see the rear of the house. There were sliding glass double doors that led to the pool deck. He saw a separate single door that likely led to the kitchen. As he expected, the blinds at the rear of the house were not drawn.

Pulling the compact binoculars from the pocket, the Marine turned contractor turned bodyguard began scanning every window for signs of movement. He found what had to be a kitchen window since through it he could make out hardwood kitchen cabinet doors. Through the glass double doors he could see a flat screen television, a couch and chairs. The second floor windows were all dark and provided no information.

After several minutes of scanning Thrasher has still not seen Beth, but he did spot a man enter the kitchen, open a cabinet and remove a glass. It was Randall Ainsley. Tommy felt a strange combination of emotions because he recognized Randy from that time he stalked Beth's Facebook page. He was happy for the positive identification, but still felt like weird having stooped to social media stalking of an old girlfriend.

Based on his movement, Randy had grabbed a bottle of something and poured it into the glass in the kitchen. He then moved out of sight but reappeared in the living room area. The light from the television glowed and Ainsley took a seat in one of the recliner chairs. That action made Tommy's radar ping hard.

Randall Ainsley was behaving, not like someone whose wife had just told him she was leaving or whose wife was packing a bag. He was acting like he was alone in the house. But, how the hell could he be alone? Thrasher crouched down in the shadows and pulled the burner phone from his pocket. Nothing, no messages or missed calls. Where the fuck is Beth? He thought beginning to feel some frustration building up. The plan was unraveling quickly. Tommy knew he needed to see the front of the house and look for Beth's car. Was it possible that she decided to cut him out, took her

SUV and left? It didn't make any sense, but anything was possible.

Thrasher moved to the far corner of the backyard where the shed was close to the stonewall fence. He could hop the wall using the shed as cover so no one in the house could see. Once in the yard he crept along the edge of the four foot high decorative wall. Tommy prayed that there was not a dog that Beth had neglected to mention.

His pulse was elevated and he took deliberate steps to control his breathing. The neighbors house was only a hundred feet away maybe a bit more. Subdivision houses were always built right on top of each other. Tommy eased around the far side of the house until he reached the corner where he could get a peek at the driveway. Both the tan Mercedes SUV and the white Nissan GT-R were parked exactly as he had seen them less than an hour before.

So she didn't leave. Then where the hell was she? Randy was drinking and watching TV like it was any night; no fighting, yelling, or lamp throwing. That was not the behavior of a man whose wife told him she was leaving him. Was she upstairs, crying in her bed because Randy forbid her to leave? "What the actual fuck?" Thrasher whispered aloud to himself.

SEVENTEEN

Tommy Thrasher retreated back to the deep shadows in the corner of the backyard where the maintenance shed and stonewall met. He continued to scan through the windows for signs of Beth. Randy had gotten up once, apparently to refill his drink, and returned to the easy chair facing the television.

Thrasher pondered his options. Should he risk trying to call the burner phone he gave Beth? The situation didn't make sense. Her car was still parked in the drive, but she was nowhere to be seen. The thought that she ran out of the house on foot seemed ludicrous. If they fought and she ran out the door, Randy would have gone after her, right? Besides, she knew where his truck would be parked. She could have ran to it in a couple of minutes.

He needed more information, a fresh angle to see into the house. Fortunately, the backyard was on the east side and the west setting sun was gone over the horizon. Tommy moved stealthily to the kitchen door and peered through at an angle; no one. He saw the half-empty bottle of Maker's Mark whiskey on the counter. That explained what Randy was drinking. Next he peered through another window. Now he could see a dining room table with four chairs. On the end of the table was Beth's purse. No way she left house without her purse, he thought.

From the corner of the double glass doors he could see the back of the recliner chair where Randy was sitting and the top of his head. Looking at the silhouette of the man, Tommy wondered what kind of character he was, what had he become? Had the addiction to painkillers and whatever else sent Ainsley over the edge? Thrasher imagined the limp body of Beth lying somewhere in the house in a pool of blood; the victim of an out of control rage of a mentally unbalanced husband.

Focus, Thrasher told himself. *Stick with the facts and information you have.* He went over a quick checklist; *Fact; Beth's car and purse are still at the house. Fact; she is nowhere to be seen. Fact; there is no sign of a fight, no broken lamps, dishes, whatever. Fact; Randall Ainsley is sitting alone in a chair getting liquored up. Fact; you don't know what the hell is going on.*

Thrasher returned to the kitchen door and gently tried the knob; locked. *Shit.* Tommy thought about picking it, but that would take some time and there very well could be a deadbolt securing the door. If he broke glass and forced his way in, Randy could very well shoot him. He did not know if Ainsley had access to a gun, he never thought to ask Beth, another mistake. Either way, he did not want to find out the answer the hard way.

There were the typical screw-in flood lamps in twin fixtures on the back of the house over the kitchen door and the glass double doors. They were not turned on, yet. Tommy imagined that they would illuminate the entire backyard area all around the pool when illuminated. At present the only light at the back of the house came from the soft blue glow of the pool lights.

There were a few outdoor lounge chairs scattered around the pool deck. As quietly as a mouse, Thrasher lifted the chairs, one by one and moved them to the far side of the deck. Without making a sound, he turned one of the chairs on its side.

Next the Marine combat veteran reached up and unscrewed the flood lamps over the kitchen door. Then, with as much stealth as he could manage, Tommy unscrewed a single flood lamp over the double glass doors. He left the lamp angled toward the pool chairs alone. Now he deliberately counted long paces from the double doors to the single kitchen door. The distance was five long paces, approximately fifteen feet perhaps a shade more. From experience, Thrasher knew that it would take him about one second, not more than 1.5 seconds to close that distance at a run. Moving at a fast paced walk it might take 2 seconds or so.

The ground from the house to the pool was covered with a decorative, stone and concrete material. It was purpose designed not to be slippery even when wet with splashed pool water. Tonight it was dry.

Thrasher picked up an aluminum and plastic pool chair, not a long lounge chair, but the other kind. He walked to the far side of the kitchen door, took a deep breath, and counted down in his head; *3, 2, 1.*

EIGHTEEN

The pool chair flew threw the air and came crashing down onto the hard deck directly into the pile of lounge chairs Tommy had set up. The noise from the aluminum and plastic was shockingly loud as it broke the still silence of the cool fall evening. It was so loud, that for a brief moment Thrasher thought it might alert the neighbors.

Within two seconds, as if on cue, the lone flood light came on illuminating the mess of chairs Tommy had created. Thrasher heard the muffled noise of one of the double glass doors sliding open. Time seemed to stand still. No one appeared. First he saw the glint of light as it reflected off of a large stainless steel revolver, then he saw the hand holding it, then an arm. *He's leading with his gun. Amateur.*

The entire form of Randall Ainsley appeared as a partially lit silhouette. He was backlit by the house lights and the flood light overhead cast his shadow on the pool deck. "Hey fucker, I have a gun. I'll blow your fucking head off." Ainsley announced to the backyard. Like a predictable animal, Randy turned and focused on the mess of chairs. That part of the deck was clearly visible and he pointed the large wheelgun in that direction.

Ainsley committed to the chair mess and took one step. Thrasher did not run, but took long rapid strides. The Glock 19 was out and in his right hand. If someone had been timing how long it took for the physically fit Military Contractor to close to his target it was 1.75 seconds.

Thrasher knew from his education that, although the frame of a Glock 19 was made of injection molded polymer and weighed next to nothing, the slide was made of hardened steel and weighed more than a pound. He also knew from reading that, unlike they did in old movies, Western lawmen, like Wyatt Earp, did not hit opponents over the head with the butts of their six guns.

Wyatt Earp used to "buffalo" drunk and belligerent bad men by laying the heavy steel barrel of his Colt 1873 revolver across the base of their skulls at an angle. Thrasher held the Glock 19 in manner so he had a rock solid grip, but no fingers were near the trigger. One pound plus of hardened steel Glock slide made contact with the right rear side of Randall Ainsley's skull.

The stainless steel revolver clattered onto the pool deck as it's owner's knees went limp and he crumpled to the ground. Thrasher recognized the blaster as a Smith & Wesson, probably a Model 66 .357 Magnum. With his right boot Tommy shuffle kicked the wheel gun hard and it splashed into the pool.

There was no time to be gentle. Thrasher grabbed his target by the back of his shirt collar and dragged him through the open sliding door and deposited him face down hard on the kitchen floor. Randy was semi-conscious and mumbling incoherently. With one swift, violent move, Thrasher grabbed the coffee maker off of the counter and ripped the cord from the back of it. *Cheap crap* he thought. The cord was only about four feet long, but it would do.

Tommy dropped a knee between Ainsley's shoulder blades. It was difficult for a fully alert man to push up against a knee to shoulders, much less one teetering on unconsciousness. When Randy's wrists were bound tightly with the coffee maker cord, Thrasher rolled him to the side, undid his black leather belt and slid it out.

Tommy dropped Ainsley into one of the wooden kitchen chairs. The chair had a high back and open area at the top. *Perfect.* Randy was starting to gather his senses. "What the fuck? Who the fuck are you? I told your boss everything was cool." Tommy ignored him and slipped the leather belt through the hole in the back of the chair and secured it around Ainsley's neck.
Randy instinctively pulled against the belt to try on stand up only to realize that he was choking himself.

For the first time Thrasher spoke. "Settle down fucker, or this will be painful." Standing in front of the bound man he stared menacingly. All Ainsley could see was Tommy's eyes as the rest of his face was hidden under the fleece balaclava. He was all black and gray from head to toe including the black shooting gloves on his hands.

"Fuck you, cocksucker!" Randy yelled. The Maker's Mark had given him some misplaced courage. "I told the other guys that we were on track. What else do you want from me?" As an act of defiance, Ainsley kicked his right leg out at the dark figure before him. The kick missed, but he successfully annoyed his captor. A black gloved fist arrived, seemingly out of nowhere, and made contact with the left side of his face. There were those bright lights again.

In the third kitchen drawer he opened, Tommy found what he was looking for, a silver roll of duct tape. *God Bless the Duct Tape company* he thought, *Every home in America has at least one roll.* Using the tape, Ainsley's legs were rapidly secured to the legs of the chair, no more kicking. For good measure, a few wraps secured Randy's torso to the wooden chair back.

Randall Ainsley was going nowhere and Tommy needed a moment to process the situation. One more piece of duct tape went across his mouth. While searching for the duct tape, Thrasher had opened a drawer full of neatly folded kitchen towels. He grabbed the a maroon colored one and wrapped it around his target's head, his eyes were covered completely. Randall Ainsley would now only see and speak when his captor wanted him to do so.

Thrasher grabbed Beth's purse and dumped it out on the table. He found her phone and it was indeed still turned off. The keys to the house and SUV were there as well. Next, he swept through the house. No signs of a struggle or a fight, no blood, and no Beth. A part of him had hoped she would be sobbing in her bedroom, he knew that was a long shot. The other part of him was relieved not to find her body. The mystery of her disappearance remained.

It was time to extract answers from the one source that would know. A drug-addicted, definitely dirty, soon to be ex-husband. Back to the kitchen Tommy went.

Ainsley's body was still, but there was the sound of heavy, labored breathing. Tommy approached from the side and grabbed the top of Randy's head pulling it upright. He leaned down and spoke slowly with the most menacing voice he could muster. His captive had to be one hundred percent convinced psychologically that he was in complete control. There was no time for a long, protracted interrogation.

"Listen to me, Tommy spoke attempting to mimic them most menacing Drill Instructor he had ever encountered, "We are all done with the bullshit. I ask questions, you answer them. Nod your head if you understand. Ainsley nodded meekly.

Thrasher removed the duct tape from his captives mouth. "Where is Beth?" he asked. Though his eyes were covered, Tommy could see the look of confusion on Randy's face. "Wait, what?" he said. For the first time Randall Ainsley considered that the person who had him duct taped to his own kitchen chair was not related to his other 'associates'.

The whiskey courage returned. Ainsley laughed loudly. "Buddy, you have seriously fucked up. You have no idea just who it is that you are fucking with." Randall shifted to a defiant tone. "I'm connected motherfucker, and you are now a dead man." Ainsley looked up blindly. "I'm connected to real hard hitting motherfuckers and you are a dead man, you hear me? You are a dead man!"

Well, it just couldn't be easy, could it? Thomas Thrasher mused to himself.

It doesn't take a hero to order men into battle. It takes a hero to be one of those men who goes into battle.

General Norman Schwarzkopf

NINETEEN

The golf course was now completely dark, no risk of being seen on the return trip to his truck. Tommy found the Dodge unmolested exactly as he had left it. He drove away from the subdivision back toward the Hilton Garden Inn. In less than a few hours, his trip to Henderson, Nevada had changed from a visit with an old flame in marital distress to something much more menacing and dangerous, more dangerous of a situation than he had imagined that he would encounter CONUS.

Before he reached his hotel, Tommy pulled into a burger joint parking lot to fire off a text to Josh.

Shit has become more complicated. Sarge good for a couple more days?

Josh responded almost immediately.

The girls will be delighted. They love that mutt. You need backup? Say the word.

Thrasher paused to consider his answer. The shit had gotten deeper than he ever thought it would get. But, did he really want to bring a friend, a teammate, into the mess he had stepped in? No, not just yet.

Good for now. Thanks for watching the mutt.

Roger was the one word response from Josh.

Tommy was once again grateful that he had friends, real pipe hitting friends that did not waste words. They trusted his judgement and he trusted theirs. Thrasher had a relationship with men that the vast majority of the American populace could not begin to comprehend. He had risked his life for others and they had done the same for him. That kind of reality was lost on the modern populace, so eaten up by image and status and personal comfort. Most American men of his age were only concerned with "how to get theirs". They were weak and distracted by sports, games, and the desire to get the most with the least amount of effort. The moment that life became difficult or uncomfortable, those in Tommy's generation quit trying or looked for someone else to blame for their problems. No one took responsibility for their lives or was willing to be uncomfortable.

Thrasher had seen the real world, the ugly, harsh, brutally violent world. With fellow Marines, and later OGA teammates, Thrasher has faced terrorists, enemy combatants, and extremist haj who wanted to bully the free world into doing as they commanded. In other parts of the world Tommy had witnessed the results of unchecked bullies; beheaded corpses in the streets, women maimed with knives or disfigured by acid for failing to kowtow to the jihadist bullies. It sickened him to think that criminal thugs and bullies were loose in the United States.

He could have turned onto the highway onramp, left the mess he found in Nevada behind, and just returned to his life in Salt Lake City. After all, this was not a sanctioned military operation, this was not an OGA assignment or contract. There would not be ribbons or awards at the end of this mission. There would be no fat contractor paycheck to justify the risks he would take.

As he drove through the darkness, Thrasher continued to process the risks versus rewards. If he pushed forward, there would be no going back. He had already crossed the "good conduct" line that he always held while CONUS. His behavior at the Ainsley home definitely put him over the line of what stateside law enforcement would consider reasonable behavior.

He needed to get back into Operational Mode and he knew it. Emotions and feelings were nice but, he needed to deal with the facts. As he pulled into the hotel parking lot, Thomas Thrasher was nearly overwhelmed with facts. He had a lot of information to process. He also realized that the clock was ticking. Beth Alexander's life was on the line and how he acted and the choices he made could determine how much longer her life would be.

Tommy did not consider himself to be a "drinker". A single glass scotch was normally his limit. Early on in his Marine career he had gotten drunk, so drunk that he ended up "time traveling". He would be one place, blackout and realize he was in another place. Tommy was out with his fellow jarheads in New Orleans on Bourbon Street. They had started the night at Pat O'Briens and were drinking Hurricanes. Hurricanes were red, fruity drinks that contained a deceptive amount of alcohol. Years later, Thrasher would joke that if it were not for the efforts of a good friend, he would still be lost somewhere in New Orleans.

The time traveling experience had taught him to go slow with the booze. Even when out with the boys, Tommy was sure to pace himself. He realized that there was no way he could have defended himself from attack or anything else that night. He had time traveled once, and once was enough.

Thrasher turned the truck around and drove back out of the parking lot, then found a liquor store. He did not know if he wanted a drink or needed one. At this point in time, he really didn't care.

TWENTY

The outdoor patio area of the Hilton Garden Inn was deserted. The temperature was cool, but not cold. Tommy wore his black hooded sweatshirt. Beside him, in a disposable heavy-paper coffee cup from his hotel room, was two fingers worth of Johnny Walker Black. A hand-rolled Dominican cigar, burned slowly in the generic black plastic ashtray. Thrasher had no intention of getting drunk, but he was appreciating the blended Scotch Whiskey. There we a spiral notebook and pen in his lap.

Now, in this moment, Thomas Thrasher was involved in mission planning. Like the innumerable mission planning briefings he had sat through as a Marine and then again later at a Military Contractor, Tommy needed to put it all together. In the Corps the acronym had been SMEAC; that stood for Situation, Mission, Execution, Administration & Logistics, Commands & Signals.

Regardless of the fact that it was just him alone, no team, Thrasher knew that he needed to SMEAC the problem. He also knew that his primary source of intelligence, Randall Ainsley, was not one hundred percent reliable. However, he did have some other information to go with, that is, what Beth had told him.

At first Ainsley had been defiant. His bravado, based upon the fact that he considered himself to be "connected" to powerful organized crime members, did not last as long as he would have hoped. Duct taped to the chair as Randy was, it was a simple task for Tommy to put him on his back and elevate his feet.

Thrasher was not an interrogator to be sure, but he knew enough about professional interrogation to understand that you could never really "beat the truth" out of someone. After so much pain, the subject would begin telling the interrogator whatever they thought that person wanted to hear. Thrasher needed real truth. A terry cloth kitchen towel and a pitcher of water had allowed him to extract great amounts of information from the captive Ainsley. The same method that enabled CIA field agents to break battle-hardened terrorists worked wonders on the soft, subdivision dwelling, Casino executive.

The Situation was this, Beth Alexander had been taken from her home by two associates of her husband. Their stated purpose was to "watch over her" while Ainsley aided them in an extremely large embezzlement / money laundering scheme at The Shining Star Casino. The men who had "encouraged" Beth to go with them had been very angry that their other associates had been shaken down by the Henderson PD the day before.

Randall Ainsley insisted that Beth would be perfectly safe as long as he stuck to the plan. The men had promised to send her home, unharmed, but they needed to be sure she did not pull another "disappearing act" as they phrased it. The associates, a large black one and a large white one, had instructed Randy to text them the minute Beth came home. They wanted to talk to both of them together to get their stories straight. He had texted them the moment she pulled into the driveway and they arrived ten minutes later. Randy swore vehemently that he had no idea that they would take her with them.

Further encouraged by the time tested and proven interrogation technique, Ainsley confessed that he had been working with an organized criminal entity for a number of years. They knew he was hooked on prescription pain pills and originally threatened him with exposure. He'd lose his Gaming License, his job, his house, everything if he was busted. He kept right on doing drugs, but they helped him avoid or pass random drug tests with clean urine.

It was not complete extorsion, Ainsley confessed. After he was in place, overseeing much of the receipts and accounting, fabricating and altering numbers, envelopes of cash were delivered on a regular basis. There was someone else as well, high up in the accounting division, that was doing something very similar. Randall swore he didn't know who, but had his suspicions.

Tommy chuckled to himself recalling the interrogation. Once Ainsley began talking, he became a fountain of information. It was as though Thrasher was his Father Confessor and Randy needed to unburden himself.

Ainsley explained that The Shining Star Casino was relatively new. Las Vegas casino properties were not expected to turn a profit for at least five years, sometimes much longer depending on the level of investment they had made, the economic climate, etc. Huge amounts of cash came and went in and out of the casino on a weekly basis. Ainsley had been coached and instructed by a man who he knew only as "the accountant". The accountant instructed him in great detail how to manipulate the books and numbers. The Shining Star had become a very popular place to launder cash and push it out the back door.

Like he was talking to a priest in a confessional booth, Randy explained that his new friends set up the regular cocaine deliveries in the parking garage. Though Tommy didn't ask or even care, Ainsley had confessed to affairs with cocktail hostesses, most recently one named Crystal.

Throughout the entire interrogation, Ainsley insisted that everything would be alright as long as he returned to work and kept on doing what had been instructed to do. They needed him, he said and they knew if they hurt Beth he'd be done, he'd be out.

Thrasher felt then, as he did now contemplating his next action, that Randall Ainsley had an overblown sense of self-importance. He was valuable right up to the moment that his organized crime friends decided that he was not anymore. They kept him happy with the cash and blow, but they would cut him loose, perhaps with a one-way trip to the vast Nevada desert, the minute he became a liability. Beth's recent erratic behavior put Randy precariously close to the line of being a liability, or worse, a threat.

The big question was just how dangerous and desperate were these thugs? Was Beth right now being interrogated and how? Thrasher started to feel frustrated and helpless, but he pushed back the feelings and reminded himself that he had no way of knowing where they had taken her. He believed Ainsley when he swore that he did not know either. They certainly would not have told him. The fact that Beth's SUV was in the drive and her purse left behind on the table indicated that she had left in a hurry. When he dumped it out her car keys and iPhone had been in it. No modern woman willingly leaves her purse or phone behind.

"Holy Shit!" Tommy said out loud to the empty courtyard. He recalled the mental image of the contents of Beth's purse dumped out on the laquered-wood, kitchen table; car keys, various forms of makeup, her iPhone, a little red leather case with a ½ ounce pepper spray, *worthless junk* he thought. But, he didn't see the small black burner phone her had given her. It wasn't in the pile on the table. Tommy felt his heart racing. Was it possible that she still had that phone on her?

It was a long shot, but Thrasher now felt like there was some hope. He let the cigar go out, finished the scotch and hustled back to his room to get on his laptop computer.

TWENTY-ONE

Tommy powered up his Macbook and the few seconds it took to login seemed much longer. He laughed at himself, how could he have missed that Beth's burner phone was not in her purse? The software program that he was about to open was not technically one-hundred percent legal in the United States. That is, it was installed by Fishstick in the command post back in Baghdad.

Fishstick, in addition to being an excellent driver and pipe-hitting shooter, was a very talented computer technician and programmer. The US Army used the "Blue Force Tracker" to keep tabs on their vehicles and personnel. Blue Force Tracking allowed Big Army to use GPS to locate and track friendly forces in theater. After the first ambush incident, Josh Kimball wanted their own in-house type of Blue Force Tracker. Fishstick had a relatively easy solution; a "find your phone" computer program.

Pay as you go, no contract phones were tremendously popular with both the civilians and insurgents in Iraq. Fishstick was able to create a software solution where they could plug in the phone number of any active mobile phone and locate it via GPS. As long as the phone was turned on, the program could use GPS to locate it within ten meters or so. Like a proud father, Fishstick and briefed the entire team on the use of what he called the "G-Force Tracker", a play on the Army's software name.

The G-Force Tracker had worked like a charm. Not only was the Detail Leader able to pinpoint the locations of all of his men in the field, there had been times when they used it to keep track of informants or "snitches".

Fishstick had installed the program on Tommy's computer as well as other team members. Thrasher never envisioned that he would need it CONUS, but he kept it for future contract assignments. Of course, an RFID bag could defeat the GPS detection, but few people who were not operators understood what the hell an RFID bag was or that they even existed.

The majority of Americans believed that putting their phone on "airplane mode" hid its location. It did not. However, turning off the phone, in most cases, would only provide the location where the phone last was when it powered down. Thrasher chuckled to himself. For most Americans, turning off their phone was equivalent to turning off a life-support system. They could not imagine it.

Calling or even texting Beth's burner phone was too risky. If she did indeed have it hidden on her person, the phone vibrating, or in the worst case ringing or pinging, would be a disaster. Tommy had to pray that the phone was turned on and that Beth had been able to keep it with her. The thugs had forced her to leave her purse behind, perhaps in their minds, separating a woman from her purse was the equivalent of searching her.

Thrasher opened up the G-Force Tracker program and typed in the number of the burner phone he had purchased and given to Beth. A spinning circle appeared on the screen to let him know that the program was working and using GPS to conduct the search. "Dear Lord, please let this work" he said aloud in a whispered tone.

TWENTY-TWO

Randall Ainsley said not one word to anyone as he made his way to his office on the second floor of The Shining Star. A couple of people attempted a morning greeting, but his eyes were focused straight ahead and down so as not to make eye contact with anyone. He walked with a quick paced and made a straight line for his office door.

With the door closed behind him, Randy dropped down into his black leather swivel chair. His mind was not on work and or the extra-legal bookkeeping that kept him in cash and cocaine. Instead, inside of Ainsley's mind there was a tornado of emotions of which he was desperately trying to get ahold.

First things first, he opened the top drawer of his desk reached in and pulled out a breath mint tin container. He kept a few Oxy in the tin for when he needed them, which was more often than not. Looking around the office for a bottle of water, but he found none. *Fuck it,* he thought and forced the pill down with a hard swallow.

Everytime he moved his head he felt the ache of the bruises at the base of his skull. His wrist bore red marks from his struggle against the coffee pot cord. He had broken free of his bonds sometime after that fucking maniac in the black mask had left him on the floor of his kitchen. He wore a long sleeved white dress shirt so the marks would remain covered, but he felt the pain when he reach out or grabbed anything. The Oxy would do the trick and relieve the physical pain.

Ainsley leaned forward and opened his brown leather attache case and pulled out the big Smith & Wesson revolver. He held it up and looked at it for a moment. Randy did not anticipate needing the gun at work, but holding it made him feel better. After freeing himself from the duct tape and electric cord he searched for the gun and fished it from the bottom of the pool. After he dried it off with a hair dryer, Randy put six fresh rounds of .357 Magnum ammunition in the cylinder. He had purchased a box of fifty when he bought the gun and still had 38 unfired cartridges left. His guess was that the pool water had ruined the six rounds that had been in the gun, so he threw them in the trash.

Never again, Ainsley thought to himself as he looked at the stainless steel handgun. No one would ever treat him again like he had been treated during the last two days. First those two goons had roughed him up, on his own turf, in the room that held so many fond memories. Then, fresh from that embarrassment, some fucking maniac in a black mask had invaded his home, tied him up and then tortured the truth out of him. *Too much,* Randy thought, *I told that lunatic way too much.*

He resolved that he would get Beth back from them. He had no idea where she was, but they needed him and that meant that they needed to keep him satisfied. They could not hurt Beth without losing him and they needed him, he continued to assure himself. While he was dressing for work his phone had buzzed. There was a text message from a number he did not recognize. It said,

She is fine. Keep your shit together. Get the job done.

Attached to the text was a picture of Beth sitting in a chair in front of a nondescript, tan colored wall. She was scowling, but it was her. Ainsley felt a mixture of anger, contempt, and helplessness all at once.

Randy had not bothered to respond. He knew who the message was from and what it meant. There was a large amount of money that needed to be moved through The Star. "The Accountant" had worked with him to put it all in motion. Ainsley told himself to get the job done and Beth would be back home. This time things would be different. He would cut back on the Oxy and coke, stay home at night and get them back to where they once were.

The big handgun was returned to the attache. Ainsley patted the top of the case knowingly. If anyone ever tried to lay a finger on him again, connected thugs or some maniac in black, he would kill them. He swore to himself that he would shoot them dead.

TWENTY-THREE

The Twin Palms Motel was a typical two-story structure with a stand alone lobby building, a communal pool and patio area. If you looked closely you could see where the Twin Palms sign had been placed over the previous signage for larger chain motel that had moved to a newer, more tourist-friendly location. The original signage had left a permanent outline on the building and the new one didn't quite cover it up.

When he was young, Tommy had asked his father what the difference was between a hotel and a motel. "At a motel, the room doors are on the outside. At a hotel, the room doors are on the inside" was the simple explanation an 8-year-old could appreciate.

The Twin Palms motel definitely fit his dad's motel description. The room doors indeed were on the outside of the motel room buildings, there were two, plus the lobby. The place seemed to be at least thirty years old. It was the type of establishment where Thrasher would say that the people in the room nextdoor were more likely than not cooking meth or servicing paying clients.

Thomas Thrasher was parked some two hundred yards away observing the entire scene through his binoculars. The Twin Palms motel was located in North Las Vegas, east of Interstate 15. This was not at all the part of Las Vegas that Hollywood writers put in their movies. The Las Vegas board of tourism did not put pictures of North Las Vegas in their ads for the city.

Gang tagging and graffiti decorated most every bus stop and desert tan concrete wall. Many, if not most of the private homes has security fences around them as well as burglar bars on the windows. This was where the G-Force Tracker software had led Tommy to; the Twin Palms motel.

G-Force was accurate within ten meters and that told Thrasher that the phone that he had given Beth was located in the south side of building #2 of the motel. What the software could not tell him was exactly which room or whether the phone was on the first floor or the second.

Good old fashioned surveillance work would be required to determine in which of the rooms Beth was being kept.

It was now nearly 6 am. G-Force had tracked the phone and given him a GPS location the night before. Tommy monitored it for movement, but after thirty minutes there had been no change. He drove from his hotel and found the Twin Palms. However, he put any idea of just jumping out of the truck and storming a motel room out of his mind. He needed to keep his emotions in check. Rash, emotional reactions could get him, Beth, or both of them killed.

You have been collecting letters again. Thrasher said to himself. *It might be time to burn them.* When PFC Thrasher had been assigned to Charlie Company, 1st Battalion, 8th Marine Regiment, the unit was in "work up" mode. The entire Regiment was scheduled for overseas deployment to the combat zone that was Iraq. Tommy had been corresponding with his family, a few friends, and a couple of girls who might end up being more than friends, since Boot Camp.

He had a resealable, clear plastic bag where he kept personal letters and photographs of family and female friends. When his Battalion shipped out he took all the letters and photos with him. He received more letters and pictures during mail calls when the unit arrived in country.

Once in Iraq, the men were given a short amount of time to acclimatize to the arid desert country and for the brass to figure out their missions. They were in a combat zone, but not yet engaged in combat.

His unit had been in country for not quite two weeks when all of the Non-Commissioned Officers and Commissioned Officers were called together for a meeting. When they returned, the Platoon Leaders gathered the men together for a mission briefing, at 0300 the next morning they would be moving out for their first direct engagement with the enemy. Squad and Fire Team leaders were instructed to ensure that every man had their weapons and gear ready.

Normally, Infantry Marines, Grunts, were loud and gregarious. When the Platoon Leader dismissed the men, no one said a word, they immediately went to work preparing. Thrasher walked silently to his cot. There was no doubt that his weapon and gear were ready, but he double checked them anyway.

Tommy pulled out the plastic bag of letters and pictures. One at a time he looked at the pictures and committed them to memory. Then, he walked over to the steel 55 gallon drum that the platoon used to burn trash. There was already a fire going inside. Tommy dropped all the letters and photos into the fire and walked away.

Before the sun rose the following day, PFC Thrasher and his fellow grunts would be engaged in real combat, not the idea of combat or training. Tommy understood that his mental focus needed to be on the mission, not on life at home thousands of miles away. If he came out on the other side alive, he would have new letters and new pictures. At that moment, the old life of Tommy Thrasher was over. What his new life had in store was yet to be determined.

Mission planning would be the key to a successful operation. He knew where Beth was, at least he knew where the phone was. That kind of intelligence put him ahead of his adversaries. There was a chance that Randy had tipped off the thugs about some lone wolf maniac dressed in black, but that chance was slim. Thrasher surmised that Ainsley would want to keep the previous night's interrogation to himself. His business partners might just decide that he was too much of a risk and cut ties with the drug-addicted casino executive if they learned he had been questioned at length.

Randy had not known or been able to give away Beth's location, so he could not have revealed it regardless. Thrasher had left Ainsley in a such state where he knew he'd be able to struggle out of the bonds eventually.

Thrasher also realized that the area around the Twin Palms was "shitty". If he tried to stake it out after midnight he would either be rousted by the local police or, just as likely, the local gang bangers would see his shiny new Dodge truck as a tempting target.

Tommy decided to continue mission planning and monitor the phone location. He had fallen asleep for a few hours in his hotel room and when he awoke around 5 am the infantryman in him had been glad for the rest. The adrenaline dump from the Ainsley house activity and the mission planning had caused the inevitable crash.

Now, Tommy was in a position to surveil his target. Even gang bangers and street hoods had to sleep, they would be crashing now and the productive people would begin their day. Most of them would head to the casinos and hotels to work as housekeepers, maintenance workers, and other jobs that paid well enough for them to live near Las Vegas, just not in the good part.

Backed in at the south end of building #2 of the Twin Palms was a new model black sedan. It was definitely nicer than any of the half-dozen other vehicles parked throughout the lot. There were a couple of white pickup trucks with ladder racks and tool boxes in the back. Obviously they were out of town construction contractors. Their occupants were the first ones to stir. Four men loaded into each truck and they were off before the sun was finished rising.

At about 630, a large black man emerged from the first floor corner room of building #2. He climbed into the black sedan and drove off alone. He was dressed in business casual, slacks and a polo shirt. Perhaps this large gentleman was a frugal businessman staying in a cheap motel to save money or perhaps he was one of the men Ainsley had described the night before.

Thrasher understood that he was playing a dangerous game and the stakes were high. There was no room for a bad guess. Adversaries had to be positively identified. He had learned that lesson and applied it time and again overseas where the enemy had stopped wearing uniforms and dressed like the non-combatants.

Within fifteen minutes the black sedan was back. The driver once again backed it in, a tactic not normally employed by frugal businessmen, but not a 100 percent indictment. When he emerged from the car, the large man carefully balanced a cardboard drink carrier with what appeared to be three large cups of coffee in one hand and a big, white, carryout bag, most likely containing fast food breakfast, in the other.

As he reached the motel room door, someone inside opened it for him and a moment later he was inside. Tommy could not see who opened the door from his angle. Now he had some real intelligence. At a minimum there were two people in the room. Through the 8x binoculars, Thrasher surmised there were at least three, maybe four large styrofoam coffee cups wedged in the drink carrier. So, it seemed likely that there were more than two people inside the bottom floor, corner room of building #2.

If Beth was indeed in that motel room, she certainly would not have been left alone when the man in the black sedan went to get breakfast. That meant at least one other suspect would be in the room with her. So, that put the head count at at least three, two suspects and Beth. Could there be a Suspect #3 in the room?

Just to reassure himself, Thrasher opened his computer and checked G-Force. The target phone was still pinging in the same location. The bad aspect about hotels or motels, from a tactical standpoint, is that the rooms as a general rule only had only one door in and out. The positive aspect, particularly from a surveillance standpoint was that there were no backdoors, no way for the occupants to slip out unseen.

Tommy began to formulate a mission plan to rescue Beth from the men who were "watching over her" as Randy had said. The situation now included two, perhaps three, bad guys, definitely armed and dangerous. Thrasher began to question his decision to turn down Josh's offer of assistance. This operation would better accomplished with a team.

TWENTY-FOUR

Gino Esposito peered out of the curtains of room 212 of the Twin Palms Motel. Room 212 was a "Deluxe" as it had a front sitting area with a pull out sofa couch and chairs. The rear part of the room held a king sized bed, bathroom and vanity. There was a microwave oven, the cheap kind with a twist knob, and a mini-fridge as well. In the center of the room a wall extended to about half of the room width giving the bedroom area semi-privacy. On the couch, Jimmy Dixon dozed, occasionally snoring aloud. Jimmy's massive frame filled what would normally be a two-person couch.

Esposito was feeling annoyed. He was sick of eating fast food take out. What he really wanted was homemade pasta and red sauce. Piero's Italian was one of his favorites in Las Vegas and he was daydreaming about their Scaloppine Parmigiana.

His current "babysitting" gig was not something he relished. Gino Esposito would normally assign something like this to someone else on the crew. He fancied himself a captain or Capo, although he had no such title in reality. The organization to which he owed allegiance did not follow strict Sicilian mafioso guidelines and structure. If he was home in his native New Jersey he would very like hold the official title of Caporegime, but Jersey was not what it once was. Gino liked Las Vegas and there was more money to be made with less hassle than back home.

It had been nearly ten years since Gino Esposito arrived in Las Vegas. He started as a "soldier", muscle, enforcer. He had proven his worth and most importantly, his loyalty, to his current employer. Years earlier Gino had been pinched and charged with assault and battery. Like a good soldier, he kept his mouth shut. Esposito ended up doing 18 months, but when he got out he was embraced back into the organization and given respect for doing his time while protecting his employer.

Gino watched the parking lot of the Twin Palms for the arrival of his employer. He had received a message advising him of the pending arrival only, no details. Esposito assumed that the discussion would be centered around what to do with the subject he was currently babysitting. Esposito could not see her from the where he stood, but he was sure that she was sulking on the bed. They had given her magazines to read. Jimmy even bought her one of those crossword puzzle books to help her pass the time. Early on, she had gotten a little too big for her britches, bitching and complaining. An open palm smack from Jimmy's giant right hand had put her back in her place.

Gino had no problem hitting a woman if he felt that they deserved it, but Jimmy was good at his job and it had established Esposito as the "good cop". She would no longer look Jimmy directly in the eye and if she wanted something she would ask Gino directly.

Right on time, a black Cadillac Escalade pulled into the lot and parked right next to their vehicle. Gino walked over to the couch and gave Jimmy a light kick. "Hey, get up the boss is here." Jimmy shook the cobwebs out and sat up straight. Gino continued, "Keep her in the back. I shouldn't be long."

Dixon got to his feet and walked to the rear of the room to check on their babysitting subject. Gino walked outside and climbed into the back of the Escalade.

TWENTY-FIVE

Hello, who are you? Tommy Thrasher thought as he watched a black Cadillac Escalade pull into the Twin Palms parking lot right in front of the room he was surveilling. Moments later a large white male, dark hair, early forties, emerged and entered the fancy SUV through the right rear door.

There was little doubt in Thrasher's mind now that Beth was in the corner room on the ground floor of building #2. Neither the late model sedan nor the shiny new Cadillac SUV fit in with the shitty neighborhood of North Las Vegas. These were not "Johns" looking for a prostitute or meth-cookers. Ainsley had told him that Beth had left with a large white man and large black man, so there they were.

It was nearly noon now and the big white guy only stayed in the Cadillac for about five minutes before he returned to the room and the Escalade pulled away. The big guy had empty hands when he exited the motel room and empty hands when he returned. Thrasher surmised that it had not been a drop off, but some kind of meeting. The windows in the Escalade were tinted so Tommy had no idea who or how many people were inside. When it pulled out of the lot, Tommy could tell there was a caucasian male at the wheel of the Escalade, but that was it. The passenger compartment was a mystery.

Thrasher began to feel some anxiety. The battery on the burner phone would die sooner than later. If they moved Beth and he lost the G-Force beacon, he might never find her in a city the size of Las Vegas. There was always the chance that they would just let her go after Randy did whatever he was supposed to do for them. There was also the very real chance that Randy would join Beth in a shallow grave in the desert as a way to clean up loose ends and eliminate witnesses. Thrasher was not a gambler and had no intention of rolling the dice over Beth's life. If they chose the desert option, Tommy did not believe they would do so in the middle of the day. Nonetheless, he was sure that he needed to accelerate the operation.

Thrasher pulled out his Glock 19 and looked at it closely paying attention to threaded barrel. *Damn, I really could use a can about now.* He mused to himself. Tommy owned a number of 'cans' as they were called in the business or suppressors as civilians referred to them. Silencers or suppressors, same thing, were perfectly legal to own in 42 of the 50 states, though they did require extra paperwork and a $200 tax. Tommy's 9mm can was locked up in a safe in Salt Lake City with his other silencers. It might as well have been on the moon.

There were other, less than legal, ways to quiet down the sound of a gunshot. Thrasher was first introduced to cans while operating as a designated marksman for the Corps. His DM rifle package had come equipped with silencer. For a sniper or designated marksman, a can was an invaluable tool. Not only did the suppressor greatly reduce the ear-splitting noise of the rifle shot, supersonic rifle shots were never really silent, a can also eliminated muzzle flash and it kept the escaping gas from kicking up a dust cloud when the shooter was prone on the ground.

Noise, flash, and dust were giveaways that betrayed a sniper's position. When Thrasher went through DM School, an abbreviated USMC Sniper School, the students had been trained to spot enemy snipers by using the noise, flash, and dust cloud to find them.

Tommy had gotten interested in the history of the silencer, it actually predated the automobile muffler. The original patent for such a device was for a "Silent Firearm" and it was filed by Hiram Percy Maxim, the son of the Maxim machine gun inventor. The junior Maxim designed the device to quiet firearms after his father had gone nearly stone deaf from gunfire noise. The first Silent Firearm was approved in 1908 and the automobile and other combustion engine mufflers mimicked that design.

During their downtime in Iraq, Tommy and Pyro had both experimented with numerous ways to quiet or mute the sound of a gunshot. Iraq was an excellent proving ground and test area for such activity. Gumball had gotten a hold of a few PSL-54 rifles.

These were the Romanians answer to the Russian Dragunov sniper rifle. The PSL-54 guns used 7.62x54R ammunition, of which there were metric tons in Iraq, and they were good mid-range rifles for a DM on overwatch. The 7.62x54R (Rimmed Russian) was essentially their version of the American .30-06 cartridge.

The problem with the PSL-54 rifles was that they were crazy loud in an urban environment and produced a considerable flash during low light. Tommy and Pyro were tasked with finding a way to suppress the Romanian long guns. The two experimented with tubing, pipes, washers and baffles. They took apart old truck and car mufflers to look inside for ideas. Pyro got ahold of several different styles of oil and fuel filters designed for SUV's and trucks and they tried them. It turned out that the fuel filters and oil filters actually did a good job quieting the big rifles. The burning gas from the rifle cartridges eventually destroyed the interior filter material, but they were disposable items so it did not matter. They would simply replace them after each use.

Back home in the United States, there were numerous fuel and oil filter thread adapters. It was absolutely taboo to use such means to quiet a gunshot, without applying for a permit and paying a tax, but desperate times called for desperate measures.

The problem that Thrasher had discovered while experimenting in Iraq was that semi-automatic pistols would not reliably cycle when quieted with auto filters. Dedicated handgun suppressors, such as the one resting in a safe in SLC, had a spring piston to ensure that a semi-automatic pistol would cycle, oil filters did not. When using such a method, the shooter would have to manually work the slide to chamber the next round.

Fuck, looks like Scylla and Charybdis again. Thrasher thought. He could either have a loud pistol that would cycle reliably or a quiet one that would essentially work as a single shot. He opened his phone and searched for the nearest auto parts store, there was one only 0.58 miles away according to GPS.

There is a time for everything,
  and a season for every activity under the
heavens:

a time to love and a time to hate,
  a time for war and a time for peace.

Ecclesiastes 3

TWENTY-SIX

"You have a dinner preference?" Gino inquired of his guest who was staring into one of the magazines they had bought her. She looked up defeated and replied "I don't really care." "Okay suit yourself, I'll let Jimmy decide, but no bitching when he comes back." She did not reply but averted her eyes from his.

Suit yourself bitch, I tried to be nice. Gino Esposito mused to himself as he turned and walked away. This would be the last meal they offered her and, according to plan, the last one she would ever eat. The boss had made the decision, she was a liability. One more text and picture update would be sent to her douchebag husband to placate him and then that would be it. Esposito had pulled Jimmy out front, away from her hearing, and told him they'd be moving out around midnight. The three of them would take a trip out into the desert but only two would be coming back.

The sun had set and Gino was hungry. Jimmy was always hungry day or night so the Capo decided to let him get whatever it was that he wanted. It was good to do the little things to keep your people happy.

Jimmy for his part was happy to get out of the room and stretch his legs. Gino watched as the sedan away, then went as sat down on the couch in the front part of room 212. Jimmy would be gone for fifteen, maybe twenty minutes or so. After a moment, Esposito climbed up off the couch and walked to the back of the room with a mobile phone in his hand.

"Smile for your loving husband." Gino said and pointed the phone at Beth. She looked up, but failed to crack the slightest hint of a smile. *No matter* he thought, *if that's the last picture you want him to have of you, fuck it.* Esposito knew that Randall Ainsley would be joining his wife as soon as the current score was completed. Losing him would put the operation back a step, but they did have another guy on the inside and old Randy had become a bit of a loose cannon.

Gino texted the words *Your blushing bride* and sent it along with the latest picture to Randall's mobile phone. He knew he was being a dick with the "loving husband" and "blushing bride" comments. *Fuck them* he reasoned to himself, *they got themselves into this mess. They should have kept their mouths shut and played the game. I hope Jimmy hurries up, I'm starving.*

Jimmy Dixon was not hurrying. Like a good driver, he stopped and filled up the car with gas. While inside he bought himself a pack of Kools, then he drove to one of his favorite take out Barbeque joints. Dixon was hungry and everything looked good. He decided to get the 3 Meat Samplers for himself and Gino, the woman would get chicken, green beans, and mashed potatoes.

They bagged it up for him in a large paper to-go bag with handles. He got a bottle of water for the woman and two extra-large yellow plastic cups of sweet tea for Gino and himself. He had his hands full balancing the drink carrier and food bag to the car. The entire way back to the motel Jimmy could smell the aroma of the chicken, pork, and beef barbeque. They had serious business to take care of later, but right now all he could think of was getting into that food.

Like a good soldier, Dixon took the time to back the car into the parking lot as he always did. The food smell was driving him wild. He had placed the drink carrier on the passenger floor area and drove carefully so the big cups of tea would not spill. With the drink carrier in his right hand and the big bag of barbeque in his left he walked slowly to the room. Gino would open the door for him.

Jimmy stopped at the door, annoyed that it was not already open. He tapped on it with is right foot and it opened a moment later. Two yellow plastic cups of sweet tea flew directly into Gino's chest. The two-hundred and eighty pound frame of Jimmy Dixon lurched forward in a strange twisted dance. The blunt end of Thomas Thrasher's stainless steel camp hatchet had made contact with the base of Jimmy's skull producing a sickening thud.

"What the fuck!?" Gino yelled in shock and surprise. Jimmy's limp body struck him as it tumbled forward, his massive frame knocking Esposito off balance. The self-appointed Capo struggled to stay on his feet and caught the image of a black clad figure following Jimmy into the room. *Blue?* Was the last thought to pass through Gino Esposito's mind as a 124 grain jacketed hollow point bullet entered his face. The copper and lead projectile pushed through his upper front teeth, shattering them, continued on clipping Gino's brain stem, and exited into the wall behind him.

Esposito slumped to the floor falling atop his companion. Thrasher pushed himself passed Jimmy's legs into the room. He had dropped the hatchet freeing up both hands to work the slide on the Glock 19. As he had practiced a thousand times, Tommy worked the slide and chambered a fresh round. It took some effort to close the motel room door, he had to push the large black man's legs out of the way. When he did so, the man's body twitched indicating life.

Thrasher leaned over and placed the blue painted oil filter six inches from base of the black thug's skull. The second shot was louder than the first one had been, but still quiet enough that no one outside of the room would peg it as a gunshot. It was a woman's scream that shook the seasoned operator out of killing mode.

Beth Ainsley stood at the back of the room screaming with a look of sheer horror on her face. Thrasher ran toward her and yelled "Beth, it's me. Stop screaming." He pulled the balaclava off of his face with one hand and placed the other over he mouth to silence her. He had dropped the Glock on the rug.

Beth's body was frozen stiff in place, her eyes wide, she was in shock from what she had just witnessed. Tommy moved her onto the edge of the bed and looked her directly at her. "We need to get out of here. Sit still and let me clean up. Do you understand?" Mrs. Randall Ainsley nodded, but said nothing.

Tommy returned to the thugs in the front of the room, with his Glock in hand. The thugs' blood was mixing with 40 ounces of spilled sweet tea and ice in the motel room carpet. The black thug was face down, the white one was on his side, eyes wide open, staring lifelessly. Thrasher had looked into the eyes of enough dead men to know this one had checked out. He had no illusion of recovering the bullets, but he did find the two spent 9mm cases and pocketed them. Tommy picked up the hatchet and set it on a wooden table next to a lamp.

Next, the operator found both of their wallets. He pulled their driver's licenses and pocketed them as well. *Intel* he reminded himself. Both men had pistols in holsters on their belts, one was a Glock 19 like his, the big black man had a SIG P226 9mm.

Thrasher knew Beth didn't have her purse, that was left behind at home. He looked around the room, in the bathroom, and on the sink counter. She had no spare clothes or personal effects. "Where is the phone, the one I gave you?" Still mute from the shock, Beth stood up and reached under her shirt. She pulled out the small black mobile phone that was hidden in her bra and handed it to him.

He took it from her, looked at the phone and then into her eyes. "This thing saved your life. Well, this thing and a guy called 'Fishstick'." Beth gave him a confused look. "I'll explain that later, right now, it's time to go."

Before he could take a step toward the door, Beth fell on him, wrapping her arms tightly around his shoulders. Her face was pressed to his chest and Tommy could hear her beginning to sob and cry. Thrasher knew they needed to get the hell away from what had become a serious crime scene, but he gave her a moment. He placed his hand gently on her head and stroked her hair. "It's okay, you are safe now. I won't let anything else happen to you."

"Yeah. That is a gun in my pants. But that doesn't mean I'm not happy to see you…"

Deadpool

TWENTY-SEVEN

"Cocksuckers." Randall Ainsley said aloud to no one in particular. In his hand he held his mobile phone and he had just received a text message, *Your blushing bride* along with a picture of a depressed looking Beth.

They had him over a barrel and he knew it. Even without holding Beth as a hostage for "safe keeping", Ainsley knew that his associates had enough dirt on him to cause him to lose his job and possibly go to jail. Of course, his associates would not want him criminally charged with anything, that would expose the deep and long running embezzlement and money laundering operation. They could expose him for the drug use and he would be finished in the casino business for a long time, if not forever.

The back to back beatings he had taken still weighed on Randy's mind. He was angry at himself for not being able to fight back, ashamed that he had been broken, not once but twice. Ainsley reached across his waist with his right hand and discreetly patted the S&W revolver he had shoved in his waistband cross-draw fashion. The stainless steel handgun was a bit bulky and heavy, but the weight was reassuring for Randy. *Never again* he thought, *never again.*

Randall Ainsley was feeling rather anxious as well. He wanted some physical relief and he had not seen Crystal since before those two goons jumped him in Room 2022. After the two goons had roughed him up, he had texted her that something had come up. Randy had left the casino and driven straight back to Henderson that night hoping to find his wife at home waiting for him. She had not been there and Randy burned a sick/personal day to sit at home and wait for her as Gino had instructed him to do.

It was after 6 pm now and Ainsley knew Crystal was down on the floor working. Randy rationalized to himself that after all that he had been put through over the last couple of days, he deserved a hard *stress relief fuck.* Being midweek, Randy was not surprised that 2022 was open, only during rare occasions did a high roller ever request that room anyway.

He fired off two texts to Crystal. First he apologized for breaking their date. Then he told her that he missed her and needed to see her tonight. The dancer turned casino hostess rarely ever turned him down, so Randy felt confident that he would be wrapping her legs around his waist not long after she clocked out.

Randy left his office and walked through the accounting area. There were over a dozen individual desks and workstations. All of the day shift people were gone and the second shift accounting department crew was only half the size of the day shift. Ainsley saw Richard Milligan leaning over one of the desks talking to a second shift clerk. *Fucking queer,* Ainsley mused nastily to himself as he walked toward the elevator.

Richard Milligan was a senior level accounting executive who had worked at The Shining Star for as long as Randall Ainsley had been there. Ainsley did not like Milligan, but tolerated him because he had to do so. The two were essentially on the same level and reported to an Executive Vice President, therefore, when Milligan came into Randy's office earlier that day with questions about the books he was working on, Ainsley could not just tell him to "fuck off". Never to his face, but among his friends at the Star, Randy referred to Richard, not Rich or Dick, Milligan insisted on the formal given name, as that "fucking queer", normally after a few whiskeys.

Randy successfully avoided making eye contact with Milligan and got into the elevator. His thoughts quickly returned to Crystal. She had not texted him back yet, but that was not a big deal. She would do it on her next break. The next scheduled coke delivery was not for a week. Randy contemplated reaching out to his associates for an early delivery, but put that idea out of his head quickly. He did not like the thought of asking for favors, not now. By his calculations, he had just enough blow for either himself or Crystal to get a good high. He would see what kind of a mood she was in. If it took offering her the last of his coke to get her naked and in bed, then so be it. He was horny as hell.

Whether or not Crystal was down to play, Randy had decided he was not going home. The thought of returning to the scene of his recent shame made his stomach ache.

TWENTY-EIGHT

Tommy did not want to frighten her more than she already was, but he knew that Beth had escaped what certainly was a fatal situation. There was no doubt in his or her mind that she needed to get away from Las Vegas, and fast. The facts before them were depressing. Beth's husband was so deep in with his "friends" that he had informed them as soon as she returned home. Supposedly they just wanted to "talk'" to her and Randy at the same time, but that did not last long.

Within five minutes of the "associates" arrival at her house, the black one produced a pistol and the white one told her that she was going with them for "safekeeping" so she did not pull a disappearing act again. Beth related to Thrasher how her husband had just stood there, speechless, while the black thug grabbed her by the arm and walked her out of the house with a gun pressed to her ribs.

Thrasher reasoned that, with her captors now room temperature, they could take the chance to retrieve clothing and personal effects from the house. It was long since dark when they approached the house, after 7 pm. Randy's car was nowhere in sight.

The house was locked and Beth did not have her keys, but she located the spare front door key that they kept hidden just in case. Tommy made sure to put gloves on his hands before entering the house, he knew, based upon Randy's criminal behavior, that sooner or later the police would come for a visit. No need to leave his fingerprints behind.

Thrasher also realized that it was also a given that the employer of the two deceased thugs would be less than happy when his handiwork was discovered. With Beth gone and no one to pin the killings on, Randall Ainsley would be suspect number one in the eyes of someone looking for payback. In Tommy's mind, Randy was a cowardly piece of shit, drug-addict. He would not lose sleep over his fate. Just the same, Tommy was not going to share those conclusions with Beth. She was a smart girl, she would come to that realization on her own.

Before they pulled into the driveway, Thrasher admonished Beth that they were on the clock. The longer they lingered in Henderson, the more danger they were in. "You have ten minutes to grab all you want to take, then we are out of there." Mrs. Ainsley knew better than to question her saviour's advice. After nine minutes and forty-five seconds they were back in the Dodge truck heading out of the subdivision.

The silver 4x4 was on I-15 heading north toward the Arizona border by 8 pm. The bright lights of Las Vegas were now in the rear view mirror. It occurred to Thrasher that he would never think of Vegas the same way again. That city had alway been a place to get away, enjoy whiskey and cigars, spend too much money, and forget about work and the horrors of war. Now, Las Vegas would be like so many other cities where Tommy had been in combat and escaped with his life.

From an operational standpoint, Thrasher knew that he needed to thoroughly debrief Beth. From a personal standpoint, she was physically and mentally exhausted. At a truck stop / gas station at the Highway 93 intersection, Tommy stopped and topped off the gas tank. He bought a couple of bottles of cold water and sandwiches for them both. Beth's barbeque dinner was all over the floor of Room 212. Before Thrasher climbed back into the truck he reached into his bag and pulled out a bottle of SWAT Fuel 9mm +P. He downed two of the blue capsules with water. The 9mm +P was a steady release, workout/energy formula. He had over five hours of night driving ahead of him and he needed his mind to be sharp and focused.

Pulling out his personal phone, Tommy sent a quick text to Josh;

Returning SLC late tonight. Be there to pick up mutt in morning. Thanks again

The reply came in a minute later.

Roger that

The current plan was to head directly to Tommy's house in West Valley, Utah. Once back in safe and familiar surroundings they would figure it out from there. At her house, Beth had grabbed the purse, personal effects, a few changes of clothes, and she had been able to raid the stash of cash that Randy kept hidden. She had nearly $4000 in hand. It would not last forever, but it was a good start.

Before they crossed the Arizona border, Beth was asleep in the front passenger seat. Tommy did not mind as he had some serious thinking to do. Traffic was light so he set the cruise control to one mile below the posted speed limit.

As he drove along the dark highway of southern Utah, Thrasher pondered the potential threat to Beth and by extension himself. Even if they were to grab Randy and squeeze him, there was little he could tell them. At first opportunity, they would need to scrub Beth's email account. Other than the burner phones, that was the only recorded communication between the two. Thrasher was glad that he had not responded to the original email and instead contacted Beth on a disposable burner. Still, he would feel safer knowing the original email was buried. But was that even possible? He knew just the person to which he would pose that question.

A grin broke across Tommy's face as he recalled the secret present that he had left Randall Ainsley.

While Beth was collecting her things, Thrasher went into the home office and found a standard white envelope. Laying the driver's licenses of the deceased thugs on the desk, he took a picture with his phone. Next Tommy slipped the ID's into the envelope, then wet and sealed it, not with his spit, but with a damp sponge from the sink. Thrasher plucked a black marker from the pen cup on the desk and placed a single "X" on the envelope face. Then he pulled opened the center desk drawer, placed the envelope all the way to the rear and closed it.

The very existence of flamethrowers proves that some time, somewhere, someone said to themselves, You know, I want to set those people over there on fire, but I'm just not close enough to get the job done.

George Carlin

TWENTY-NINE

As they drove along I-15 in the darkness, Thrasher thought about all that had transpired during just a couple of days. In his mind he could see the images of the dead men in the motel room. Tommy felt no real guilt or remorse. The thugs were dangerous and bad men, there was no doubt. Thrasher had killed bad men before, just not in CONUS. Killing villains within the borders of the United States was a new experience for him.

He kept the radio turned down so that it would not keep Beth awake, but there was just enough sound to break up the empty silence of the truck rolling down the highway. Thrasher's mind drifted back to his first deployment to Iraq with 2nd Marine Division and the first human being he had been forced to kill.

Shortly after checking in to Charlie Company, 1st Battalion, 8th Marines on Camp Lejeune the Company First Sergeant stood in front of the morning formation and called out a list of names. If your name was called, the 1st Sgt said, you were to see him immediately after formation.

Thrasher and eight other men had been called by name. As a brand new Private First Class, Tommy was a bit apprehensive as to why his name had been called. He assumed that he'd be sent on a working party or some such task. To his relief, the

1st Sgt explained that every name he called had qualified as a "Expert" marksman with the M16 rifle. Tommy had been proud to wear the Expert badge on his service uniform after Boot Camp Graduation.

The battalion needed men for the Designated Marksman program. All the enlisted men in the company with an Expert rating would be sent to DM School on Lejeune, an abbreviated form of the famous USMC Sniper School. "You won't be a fucking sniper and I better never hear you calling yourself one." the 1st Sgt admonished the group of Marines standing around him. In the Marine Corps, the term "sniper" was highly coveted. Ever since the legendary Carlos Hathcock, the billet of Sniper was viewed with awe and respect by grunts in the Infantry.

Tommy went on to graduate as the second highest shooter in his DM class. He missed the top spot by one point and frequently kicked himself over that fact. When 1/8 deployed to Iraq, Thrasher was indeed one of a handful of qualified Designated Marksmen in Charlie Company.

Once on the ground in Iraq, it did not take long before the battalion was engaged in combat operations. Thrasher and his spotter, a Lance Corporal named McIntire, were stationed a top a two story building in a village called Halabs near Al-Fallujah. Insurgents had been actively mining the roads in the area and ambushing coalition vehicles.

Two Marines in their sister company, Bravo, had recently been killed by a roadside bomb. This mission was very personal for all involved.

Thrasher and McIntire were set as overwatch for the platoon that was clearing a neighborhood and looking for a known insurgent leader, supposedly in the area. This was the third time they had set up in such a fashion and Tommy had not yet fired a shot.

In normal tactical fashion, the platoon was moving one squad at a time in a bounding overwatch pattern. McIntire, the senior man, had the radio and was in direct communication with the Platoon Leader, a 1st Lieutenant.

McIntire used a set of 10x binos and was actively scanning the area around and ahead of the rifle squads as they moved from building to building. Thrasher was laying behind a precision-tuned M16A4 rifle and looking through a 4x ACOG scope. He was wondering if this mission go off without incident like the previous two had when McIntire said "I've got something." The hair on the back of Thrasher's neck stood up.

"Three hundred meters, maybe three-fifty, at one o'clock. Two story building. There is a big TV antenna on the east side. I just saw a head poke up. McIntire directed Thrasher. "Check that, I saw another one. That's two heads. You got 'em?"

Tommy could feel his pulse increasing and took two deep breaths to calm himself. It only took a couple of seconds for him to locate the building and the rooftop. Through the riflescope he saw two dark images from the neck up, their faces were wrapped in the black scarves that the insurgents like to wear. "I'm on them." Thrasher assured his spotter.

McIntire set the binos down and picked up the handheld radio. "Charlie Two, this is Raven" McIntire called the Platoon Leader on the ground. The Lance Corporal radio man handed the handset to the Lieutenant. "Raven, Charlie Two, go ahead." "Charlie Two, be advised two potential tangos, 350 meters, roof top, watching you." "Roger that Raven, do you see…"

Before the Lieutenant could finish his question, a rifle shot broke from Thrasher's M16. Then another. "Shit!" McIntire yelled. "I saw an RPG, I saw an RPG!" Tommy realized he was talking loud and fast. He took another deep breath. He was still glued to the rifle stock and his eyes had not left the rooftop. "Charlie Two, Raven. Tangos engaged. RPG spotted repeat, RPG spotted."

The grunts on the ground had gone into immediate action mode. They took cover with rifles and machine-guns pointing outward. The Platoon Leader quickly ordered two squads to provide cover and watch for ambush. Then, with McIntire's guidance via radio, the Lieutenant led one squad to take down the building in question.

Neither Thrasher or McIntire took their eyes off of the rooftop or the building. McIntire had the binos to his eyes again. "I hope for both of our sakes you really saw an RPG, or some kind of weapon. If not we're both fucked."

For a moment Tommy began to doubt himself. It all happened so fast. McIntire was making the radio call when the two dark figures popped up. One had a launcher on his shoulder. It was only a second or two between when he saw the bad guys and he fired his rifle. Tommy didn't remember sweeping off the safety. It was as if his body was on auto-pilot, it knew what to do and did it.

Shortly, the DM team heard the sound of muffled rifle shots. They knew that they were coming from inside the target building. The actual time lapse was only a few minutes, but it seemed much longer. Then, men in familiar desert digital, camouflage uniforms appeared on the roof. Tommy put the rifle on safe and shifted the muzzle away from the friendly troops.

"Raven, Charlie Two. The Platoon Leader broke radio protocol and did not wait for response. "We have two dead tangos on the roof, two more in the house. Good job, Marines. We owe you guys."

Thrasher smiled into the darkness as he drove down highway 15. The Platoon Leader had found an RPG launcher and six rockets on the roof along with two AK-47's. Tommy's DM team had put down insurgents and prevented what could have been a deadly ambush. The Lieutenant had put both McIntire and him up for the Bronze Star, but the Battalion Commander decided that Letters of Commendation would suffice.

"Fucking officers." Thrasher said aloud and laughed. Beth stirred at the sound of his voice but did not wake up. Recalling the details like it was yesterday, the RPG gunner had taken a 5.56mm bullet to the head. The gunner's partner had started to move away and caught the second round Tommy had fired right under the jawline.

McIntire and Thrasher never saw the results of their handywork, but the men of 2nd Platoon, Charlie Company, who took down the building, spread the word about how their DM team, and Thrasher in particular, were stone killers. In the eyes of his fellow grunts, PFC Thrasher went from being an FNG (fucking new guy) to a "salt". From then on the men of Charlie Company felt confidence knowing that Raven was watching their backs.

Cowards die many times before their deaths; the valiant never taste of death but once.

William Shakespeare

THIRTY

Sergeant Robert Morrison had been on the North Las Vegas Police Department for twelve years. He had done his time on patrol, worked hundreds of midnight shifts and earned his spot on the Detective Bureau Homicide Division. Morrison had seen so many dead junkies and hookers that he doubted he could remember them all. Gang killings, drive-bys and drug deals gone bad were commonplace. However, this crime scene had his professional interested piqued.

It was just after 11 am. Housekeeping had entered room 212 shortly after 9 am. The 911 call had come in to the North Las Vegas Police Dispatch at exactly 0921. A frantic hispanic woman had given the dispatcher enough information to know that two men appeared to be dead at the Twin Palms motel. The arriving patrol unit secured the scene and called for homicide detectives.

"Well, what is your take on this." Morrison asked his partner Franco Silvio. The junior man had been with Homicide only nine months. "Drug deal gone bad maybe?" Silvio offered. "Not likely, these two are not meth-pushers, they are connected. Neither one had ID but I recognize the white one, that's Gino Esposito, or at least it was. He is a 'known associate' of Robert Sullivan. That name ring a bell?"

Detective Silvio shook his head. Morrison took the opportunity to school his apprentice. "Robert, 'Bobby' Sullivan is one of our leading local organized crime figures. The white corpse with the bullet hole in his face is a known associate of Sullivan. Esposito was not a street level pusher, he is, or was, a captain or Capo in mafioso lingo. This could be a rival mob hit, but it sure as shit was not some kind of dope deal gone wrong. Do you think dopers would have left their victims' guns behind? And who the fuck orders take-out Barbeque in the middle of a dope deal?"

Franco shugged and Morrison continued, "When we get the ID back on the giant black one, $100 bucks says he connected to Sullivan in some way. The car is registered to an anonymous sounding car company. My bet is that it is tied to one of Sullivan's legitimate business ventures. Also, we haven't found any shell cases. That means the killer or killers used a revolver or they took the cases with them. That's not doper behavior."

"If I didn't know any better, I'd think you were excited by this case." Silvio offered. "Kid, after you've worked a hundred dead hookers and junkies, you will look at a case like this with professional intrigue too."

The photographer from the forensic team walked out of the room and addressed Sgt. Morrison. "I'm finished here." he said. "Okay, Morrison said aloud for all to hear, "let's get them bagged up."

Pulling Silvio to the side, Sergeant Robert Morrison offered grimly, "If this was a mob hit, and I'm betting it was, those two bodies are only the first of many to come."

THIRTY-ONE

"God dammit!" Bobby Sullivan exclaimed as he slammed the telephone handset down onto the receiver on his desk. He did not do it often, but Sullivan appreciated having a traditional desk phone that allowed him to execute that physical act of frustration.

The person on the other end of the line, one of his lieutenants, had just informed him the North Las Vegas PD discovered and removed the bodies of Gino Esposito and Jimmy Dixon from the Twin Palms Motel. Esposito was supposed to send a message letting Sullivan know when the job with the woman was finished. No message had come and Bobby had feared something was wrong. Gino was a loyal captain and was not one to fuck up an assignment.

According to the caller, a detective from NLVPD showed up at Superior Automotive, one of Sullivan's legit businesses, to tell them they had impounded a car registered to Superior Auto and to make inquiries about Esposito and Dixon. Like a good man, the manager on duty had informed the detective that they leased cars to many people. He was not privy to their backgrounds or behavior. The manager had even pressed the cop about getting the car back.

Sullivan stood up and moved out from behind his desk. Walking to the window he stood and looked out at the Strip, Las Vegas Boulevard. His office offered him an excellent view of the shiny casino buildings and bright lights. Bobby stared for a moment at the city. He could not honestly say that it was "his city", but he felt very strongly that he owned and controlled a good part of it.

Gino Esposito had been tipped by one their dealers about Randall Ainsley. Randy was a tool to be used to further their off the books casino ventures. Ainsley had worked out and all was going as well as could be expected right up until recently. Now, the entire thing was going to shit, fast.

The wife had gotten agitated and suspicious. At first it seemed that she could be plactated with spending money from her husband. In Sullivan's experience, wives and girlfriends were apt to look the other way when a steady stream of cash was available for shopping trips to the high end designer shops that Vegas offered. All the major players in high fashion had retail stores in Las Vegas, primarily located on the busiest parts of the strip.

Bobby himself had a steady girlfriend and a couple of other, not so steady but, willing women to occupy his nights. The steady one, Maria, was wise enough not to question him about his business activities. Sullivan was fond of Maria as fond as any of the numerous others that had come before. She liked shoes and clothes and squealed with joy when Bobby would treat her to a shopping trip on Las Vegas Boulevard.

So the wife, Sullivan was pretty sure her name was Beth, had become not only a pain, but a threat to jeopardize the operation they were running with her oxy-addicted husband. The executive decision had been made to remove her from the picture, get through the current money moving scheme and then remove the husband as well. Ainsley did not know everything, but he knew enough to put a hurt on the business if the cops picked him up and squeezed him.

"Shit", Sullivan said aloud to his empty office as he looked out the window. Two of his best men were in the morgue and no word about the woman. Bobby had to assume that she was in the wind now. The biggest questions were who and how. Who the fuck had the balls to cross him and take down his men, skilled and dangerous men? And, how in the fuck did they know where to find them and the wife?

Bobby Sullivan allowed himself to entertain the idea that he might have underestimated Ainsley. Did that son of a bitch cut a deal with a competing organization? Had that organization rewarded him by picking up his wife and killing Gino and Jimmy? If that was the case, who out there had the elephant sized balls to cross him? Were husband and wife right now planning to flee Las Vegas? Had they already done so? *Too many unanswered questions. I need real answers.* The crime boss said to himself.

Sullivan was relieved when he heard a knock on his office door. "Come." he yelled. Craig Rowland, one of his lieutenants entered the room. Sullivan didn't waste words. "Grab some men and find that fuck Ainsley. Keep him breathing. We have questions for him."

Rowland nodded and waited dutifully to be sure his boss was finished speaking. "One of our girls spent last night with him at The Star. He was still at the casino when she left him just before eight this morning." "That is the best news I have heard all morning, Craig." Sullivan said, relieved to know that Ainsley had not fled during the night.

However, that fact led to more questions. Why, if his wife was missing from the motel, would Ainsley spend the night with another woman in a suite at the casino? "You are absolutely sure he stayed the night in town?" Sullivan asked for clarification. "Crystal has never lied to us before. We've been using her to keep tabs on Ainsley since he started banging her several months ago. I don't see why she'd start lying now."

"You're a good man, Rowland. Sullivan praised his subordinate. "Top priority is to put hands on that fuck. Let me know the moment you have him on ice." "What about the other one, the sissy?" Rowland inquired. "Mr. Milligan seems to be performing as expected. Let's assume for now that he is up to the task." Craig Rowland, nodded his understanding and removed himself from the office.

THIRTY-TWO

The silver Dodge 2500 had pulled up in front of the Thrasher house in West Valley, Utah just before 2am. Tommy was grateful for their late arrival as he would be able to usher Beth into the house without the likelihood of nosey neighbors seeing her. She might not like it, but Beth was going to be in sort of witness protection until he could get a better handle on just who it was that had taken her.

Thrasher escorted Beth to his bedroom. The second bedroom in the house had been converted to his office. She was still exhausted from her ordeal, but her mood seemed to lighten. Beth had slept in the truck until they had passed Provo and were nearly to SLC. "So this is your room?" she said with a smile. "Yep all mine. Why, what did you expect?" "I don't know, a cot and milk crates." She was teasing him so her mood had definitely improved.

"I keep this room for guests, normally I sleep in the backyard under a poncho." Two could play the smart ass game. "You know I was just kidding you. Beth replied, a bit more demure. "The bed is wonderful. I bet it is comfy." "Get settled, Thrasher said "I'll take the couch and we'll figure something out in the morning."

Beth looked down at the floor for a moment and then up at Tommy. "I really wish you wouldn't.

Please, stay in here with me. I don't know if I could stand to be alone right now." Thrasher did not protest. She had been through more psychological trauma than most people ever have to deal with during the past few days. He showed her to the master bath just off of his room and told her he would secure the house and be back.

Tommy double-checked the doors, set the alarm, and did a complete walkthrough of the house. Within five minutes or so he was back in the room. Beth was in bed, under the covers with a sheet and blanket pulled up to her neck. She smiled at him but did not speak.

Thrasher turned out the bedroom light. The curtains were parted a bit and the moonlight came through the window. It was just enough to make out shadows and silhouettes. Tommy undressed at the edge of the bed and set his pistol on the nightstand in the holster as he normally did.

As he climbed into the bed, Beth spoke. "I'm sorry." she said. "For what?" "For the way things ended with us, all those years ago." Tommy chuckled a bit. "You don't need to apologize for that. We were young. That was a long, long time ago." "Well, I'm sorry for getting you into this mess." she continued.

Thrasher let out a deep breath. "We played the cards we were dealt. When the sun comes up we'll address that situation. For now, I don't want to talk about it anymore. We both need some rest."

It was true. Tommy was mentally as well as a bit physically exhausted. The boost from the SWAT Fuel had worn off and he was grateful to be in his own bed again. Before he had finished speaking, Beth had found him under the covers. She touched his bare chest first with her hand and then slid up to him, draping one of her legs over his.

Thrasher knew in a moment that Beth was completely naked. As she wrapped herself around him he could feel the warmth between her legs pressed to his muscular thigh. Her soft and wonderful bosom was cuddled against him. Beth reached down and felt the cotton boxer briefs he was still wearing. "I really don't think you will be needing these." she cooed softly into his ear. Tommy obliged her and lifted his midsection off of the bed. She slipped the briefs off and tossed them into the darkness.

"I really can't repay you for all you have done for me. Beth whispered close enough to his ear that Tommy felt her warm breath and it stirred him sensually from head to toe. Before he could reply she placed a finger to his lips. "Lay still and let me start thanking you now."

THIRTY-THREE

Craig Rowland enlisted a couple of Sullivan's soldiers to help him and headed to The Shining Star. His informant had assured him that Randall Ainsley was indeed at work. Rowland was pleased to have that information, but he understood that he could not simply waltz into a busy casino and grab Ainsley. He would have to be patient and wait for an opportunity to grab him away from witnesses.

It did not take long to locate Randy's sports car in the executive portion of the employee parking area. Rowland explained to his associates that they would be patient and wait. Nonetheless, he did not want Ainsley slipping out and leaving his car behind. One of the two thugs was sent inside to keep an eye on the office area. Rowland sent a message to Richard Milligan advising him to let him know the moment Ainsley left the accounting floor.

Rowland thought about sending an update to his boss, but then decided not to bother him with the details. Sullivan had instructed him let him know when Ainsley was on ice. That much was clear. A man like Bobby Sullivan was a busy person and Rowland did not want to risk bothering him.

Patience the lieutenant reminded himself. *We'll have that fuck soon enough.* Rowland was a good lieutenant and understood not to hurt the man too badly before given further instructions. Regardless,

Gino Esposito was a friend. Rowland felt certain that Ainsley was involved somehow in his friend's death. He was very much looking forward to the chance to make the accountant pay.

Rowland had the spot picked out where they would hold Ainsley until they had further instructions. Sullivan owned a storage warehouse not quite two miles away. The warehouse was filled with old and outdated slot machines and casino furniture. The contents were too dated for Las Vegas, but several Indian casinos, located all over the west, would frequently buy the machines and other furnishings.

Randall Ainsley was at his desk. His thoughts were all over the map. Crystal had not disappointed him the previous night. He had given her the last of his coke and satisfied himself with whiskey. They fucked furiously and he had slept until nearly eight in the morning. However, despite the carnal romp, Randy was anxious. He must have looked at his phone a hundred times already and it was just now after noon.

There had been no updates or instructions from Gino. No smartass texts like the "blushing bride" comment from the night before. No pictures of Beth frowning and looking annoyed, nothing.

A dozen times Randy picked up his phone to send a text to Gino's number. But, every time he had stopped himself. What would he say? The thugs had him over a barrel. If he contacted them it would more likely than not piss them off. He was supposed to be busy altering the books and adjusting the receipts as he had done so many times before, but he kept getting distracted. The coke was gone and he had doubled up on the oxy. Ainsley realized that he was out of spare clothes and accepted the fact that, whether he wanted to or not, he would have to drive back to Henderson. No playtime with Crystal tonight.

Randy had tried to keep himself all day. That *fucking queer* Milligan had knocked on his door and interrupted him with some bullshit question. Randy gave him a one word answer and told him he was busy and to "fuck off". Ainsley knew he could get into some trouble for yelling at Milligan in a crowded office, but he was beyond caring.

At half past 3 pm, Randy could not take anymore. His nerves were shot. He needed to get out of the office. The books and all the bullshit would be there for him the next morning. Ainsley grabbed his briefcase, said nothing to anyone, and headed for the elevators.

Rowland's phone vibrated and he picked it up *He's coming* was the message he received from the man inside. The thugs' car was backed into a spot across from Ainsley's white Nissan GT-R. "Wait for him to walk by, then get out and grab him. Rowland instructed his soldier. The man, Desmond, nodded his understanding. "Stuff him in the back seat. Ricky will be close behind and we'll go straight to the slot machine warehouse."

Less than two minutes later, Randall Ainsley appeared. Nervously, he looked left and right and then began walking at a fast pace, straight for his car. Ainsley did see the two men watching him, but when Desmond opened the passenger side door it banged into the adjacent car. "Shit." Rowland muttered.

Ainsley's head spun around quickly. Desmond was on his feet and moving in Randy's direction. The two men locked eyes. "Stop right there." the thug barked at his prey and picked up the pace to close on him.

Randy dropped his briefcase. Rowland was looking at Ainsley's face and saw in an instant his expression change from one of surprise to a maniacal scowl. *Oh fuck!* Rowland thought reaching for his door handle. Before Desmond could close the gap, Randy had reached across his waist and pulled out a big, stainless steel handgun.The two men were only three feet apart when the Smith & Wesson .357 Magnum revolver roared. The sound of the magnum gunshot sounded like a bomb as the noise echoed off the low parking garage ceiling.

Desmond screamed in agony and crumpled to the ground. Randy had fired from his waistline. The .357 slug entered the thug's pelvis and smashed through his right hip bone. "Fuck, fuck, fuck." Rowland said as he rapidly exited the driver's side simultaneously drawing his concealed pistol.

Randy watched the man before him fall and heard him scream in agony. "Yeah, motherfucker, not this time, not this time!" Ainsley's adrenaline had dumped. They would not take him again, not like before. He composed himself for a quick second and began to take careful aim at the face of the wounded man who was looking up at him in shock.

Before Randy could stroke the double-action trigger for another shot, two bullets struck his chest in rapid succession. For a brief moment, Ainsley thought someone had snuck up and punched him. The adrenaline was masking most of the pain. Randy stumbled a bit and shook his head violently to gain composure then saw the image of a second man closing on him. "Not this time!" Randall Ainsley tried to shout, but the words seemed muffled to his ears. He pulled up the revolver to take a shot at the new threat. At that moment a bullet from Craig Rowland's pistol caught him in the throat. The copper jacketed projectile passed through Ainsley's neck clipping one of his jugular veins.

Randall Ainsley fell back and collapsed onto the hard parking lot deck. His right lung was punctured and his chest cavity was filling with blood. Unable to produce sound, he stared at the white ceiling lights and silently mouthed the words "not this time". Then the darkness came and Randall Ainsley would say no more.

THIRTY-FOUR

Tommy Thrasher was up and awake before Beth. She was sound asleep as he quietly slipped out of the bedroom to start the coffee. Even though it was nearly 3 a.m. before he had fallen asleep, his internal alarm had gone off just after 7. Standing alone in the kitchen in only his boxer briefs, Tommy smiled. They had made love hungrily without either one saying a word.

When the pot had finished brewing, Thrasher walked carefully back to the bedroom with two full cups of coffee in hand. Setting both cups down on the nightstand, Tommy sat down on the bed next to Beth. She stirred a bit when she felt the bed move. He reached over and touched her shoulder. "Okay sunshine, I have to go get my dog."

Beth opened up her eyes and smiled at him. "Did you say 'get your dog'?" Thrasher laughed. "Yes, his name is Sarge and he's been staying with friends. I told them I'd pick him up this morning. You don't have to get up, but I wanted to let you know I'd be gone for an hour or so."

She sat up in bed and this time did not bother to cover herself with the sheet. Tommy slowly handed her a cup of coffee and was sure she had control of it before he let go. Though he did not turn away, Tommy tried not to focus on Beth's soft, pink, wonderful breasts. He had re-acquainted himself with them only a few hours before and he very much wanted renew their relationship, but not now. Now was time for business.

Looking into his eyes knowingly, Beth said "They have missed your touch. I have missed your touch." Thrasher knew she would not protest if he jumped back into the bed, but he was not being glib when he said he had to go. Tommy leaned in and kissed her on the forehead. Then he stood up. "Take your time. Drink your coffee. Help yourself to anything in the fridge. Just do not call or contact anyone. Okay?" "Yes, sir." Beth saluted with her empty hand.

Thrasher grabbed his clothes and pistol and was out the door in ten minutes. Sarge would be glad to see him. That was the great thing about dogs, no matter how long or short you were gone, they were always glad to see you.

"How'd it go?" Josh Kimball inquired as Thrasher walked through his front door. At that moment Sarge ran up, wagging his tail wildly and offering his head to be petted. Simultaneously, Tommy greeted his canine friend and answered his human friend. "Good and bad, but I'm none the worse for wear."

"Okay, hero. Josh responded. Thrasher laughed out loud. Army NCO's loved to refer to enlisted men as *hero* or *turbo*. "I have a wilderness survival class coming up next month and I could use another instructor, you have the time?" "Right now, I'll say yes. Give me the exact dates and I'll put it on the schedule."

Josh and Tommy spent another thirty minutes talking business and bullshit. Thrasher did not want to rush off, but he was anxious to get back to Beth. He did not feel entirely comfortable leaving her alone, not now.

Upon returning home Tommy found Beth in the kitchen making breakfast. She was wearing one of his T-shirts and had a pair of his slippers on her feet. The shirt hung down just far enough to cover her round bottom and her legs were bare. When Sarge rushed up to meet her, Beth bent down to pet him and rub his ears.

"Beth, this is Sarge. Sarge this is Beth." Thrasher made formal introductions realizing the entire time it was ridiculous. "He's a sweetheart." Beth said while rubbing Sarge's head and patting his belly. "If you make him a couple of eggs, he'll be your friend for life." Tommy offered. "Deal." she replied.

"Sit down and relax. I'm almost finished." Beth instructed. Tommy complied and sat down at the kitchen table. He watched her maneuvering around the kitchen and smiled broadly. "Surprised that I still cook?" she asked, catching him looking at her. "No, not surprised, just amazed that you are standing there."

He was not just being funny. As Thomas Thrasher watched his lover, from what seemed like a different life, standing in his kitchen he was indeed struck by just how strange and amazing the scene was indeed. A week prior he would have never thought he would see Beth Alexander again in his life. Thrasher was wise enough to know that they could not just forget all that had happened and start playing house together. There were still a great many questions to be answered and issues that needed attention. Nevertheless, at least for now, he would allow himself to enjoy this pleasant moment.

About the Author

Nicolas Orr is the nom de plume for a civilized barbarian, a savage gentleman, with thirty plus years of operational and combat experience in the United States and overseas. The author has carried a gun during innumerable assignments worldwide as a member of the United States Military, as a Military Contractor, and Executive Protection Agent. Though this is a work of fiction, the circumstances are based upon three decades of real world experience.

As with any work of fiction; the names, characters, businesses, places, events, locales, and incidents are either the products of the author's imagination or used in a fictitious manner. Any resemblance to actual persons, living or dead, or actual events is purely coincidental

...as far as you know.

Made in the USA
Middletown, DE
30 July 2023